I0604001

Cynthia Hickey

# Coral Shadows

## Colors of Evil, Book 2

## By Cynthia Hickey

# DEDICATION

To those who waited so patiently for book two

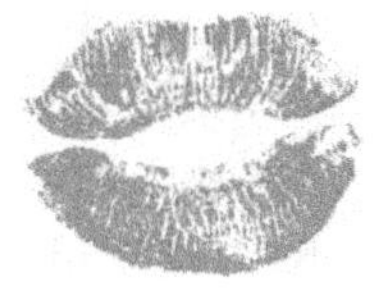

# Chapter One

Aislinn McFarland clutched her aluminum forensic case and stared at the imposing salmon-colored, stucco-plastered giant before her. Yellow crime tape fluttered in the summer breeze of Northern California.

The house towered above the other homes in the neighborhood, and her resolve to enter faltered. Not because of the smell of death emanating from the front door, but because of a feeling of not having been invited into such a place, a place of being unworthy among such wealth. The feeling of intrusion rose above the summer sun, beating on her head as perspiration beaded on her brow. She sighed, breathing in the humid air and shrugged away the unwelcome feeling.

A young male reporter loped in her direction, microphone clutched in one hand, his mouth open in preparation for a bombardment of questions. He stopped abruptly at one cold glance from Linn and snapped his mouth closed.

"I just got here, Alan," she tossed over her shoulder as she climbed the stairs. "Give me a moment to get my bearings before you pester me."

Alan Barker, zealous for news, frowned. "Talk to me when you're ready. I'll wait right here."

"Linn?" Her partner Steve appeared at her side. "You ready?"

Nodding, Linn dug into her pocket for the metal tin of scented cream she'd stashed there. She set her case on the flagstone walkway and twisted the cap off the container. She stuck her finger in the waxy balm, then spread it across her upper lip. She sighed as the smell of roses helped mask the odor of decay. "Has the medical examiner arrived?"

"He's waiting for you." Steve lifted Linn's case, grasped her by the elbow, and steered her inside the mammoth front entrance.

"Who secured the scene?"

"I did." Steve pushed open one side of the massive double, oak doors.

Although the home was chilled from air conditioning, the heavy odor of death slapped Linn in the face as she stepped into the marble-tiled foyer. She pressed her lips together, breathing through her nose the mix of decaying flesh and roses.

"Aren't you glad you added forensics to your job title? You work more with the Crime Scene Investigation now than you did as a detective."

Her gaze flicked to Steve as her mouth twitched. "Very true. I knew those extra classes would come in handy. After our run-in with Lyman, I figured I might as well. I was doing the job without the title anyway. Where's the victim?"

"Living room."

"Anyone taking pictures?"

"I took a few. You can take the rest."

Two police officers stepped aside as Linn and Steve entered, allowing them access to the scene. An over-sized, stark-white brick fireplace occupied one wall. Equally white furniture was placed at pleasing angles around a marble-top coffee table.

The victim lay face down on a faux-bear skin rug, an overturned wineglass beside a clenched fist. An empty wine bottle rested on the glass-topped coffee table.

"Detective McFarland?"

Linn set her case on the floor and extended her right hand. "Mr. Mason. What can you tell me?"

Brown eyes in a round, ruddy face turned toward the body. "There doesn't seem to be any foul play. Doesn't look like a suicide either."

"No, it doesn't. But we've only had a glance, haven't we?" Linn squatted and opened her case, withdrawing a pair of rubber gloves. She snapped them over her hands. "How long has he been dead?"

"Approximately twenty-four hours. The man's secretary found him. She came checking when he didn't show up for work. According to her, he's a workaholic. Never misses a day."

Linn turned the head and stared into the gray face of a man around his mid-fifties. He wore an old-fashioned, silk smoking jacket and nothing else. Muscular legs stuck out from beneath the hem of the jacket.

Turning, she lifted the wineglass from its nest in the long hair of the rug. Light bounced off the etched crystal. Linn raised the glass to her nose, trying to decipher a smell through the death and roses. Merlot and something…else. She wrinkled her nose and set the glass back where she'd found it. "Can we roll him over?"

"Sure." Mr. Mason grabbed the victim's shoulders and rolled him.

Linn stood staring down at the gap in the man's robe. A reddish imprint of lipsick shone up from the concave spot just above the collarbone. "Seems Mr. Vandergiven was on a date, and you're going to have to do an autopsy."

"Is that so? I was going fishing this weekend. I was

hoping to rule his death as a heart attack or something just as easy."

"Nothing that easy, I'm afraid." Linn reached for the camera around her neck and began snapping pictures of the victim and the wineglass.

Mr. Mason squatted, tracing a finger over the lip print on the glass. "My wife wears this shade. I think it's called Coral Sunset or something silly like that. Looks like a shade of orange or pink to me. Half the women in this town probably wear that same shade."

"I hope not. It'll make our job a whole lot harder. We need to question the woman he spent the evening with." Linn glanced to where Steve waited beside the other officers. "Where's the secretary?"

He motioned his head. "Crying in the kitchen. Her name is Leslie Baker."

Linn led the way to the kitchen, pulling off the gloves. Steve followed. He carried a small notepad and leaned against the doorframe as Linn approached the kitchen table.

Leslie Baker sat hunched over a pile of shredded Kleenex, her bleached-blonde head lowered as sobs shook her body. The woman raised red-rimmed, blue eyes as Linn entered the chrome appliance-filled kitchen. Linn's whole house would fit in this one room.

With a sigh, she lowered herself into a metal chair across from the distraught woman and reached for a tissue. She swiped it across her mouth, removing the rose-scented lotion. "Ms. Baker?"

"Yes." The woman sniffed.

"How long have you worked for Mr. Vandergiven?"

"Almost six months. He is, was, a wonderful man. Always gave me gifts, letting me take time off. He wasn't a very demanding boss. I can't believe he's dead."

Linn leaned forward, her elbows resting on the tabletop. "It appears as if your boss had a lady friend the night he died. Would you know anything about that?"

"A lady friend? That's impossible." Leslie straightened in her chair. Her eyes focused on Linn.

Why?"

"Because…Uh…" Leslie grabbed for another Kleenex. "We were keeping this low-key, but…David and I were, you know, seeing each other." Fresh cries erupted from the woman's mouth.

*Hence the gifts.* Linn glanced to where Steve wrote on his pad, the pen scratching out notes. "What shade of lipstick do you wear, Leslie?"

"What?"

"Your lipstick. What color is it?"

Leslie dug through the pile of Kleenexes, showing Linn one with a lipstick smear. "I…mauve, I guess. I change my lipstick to match what I'm wearing. Why?"

"When was the last time you saw Mr. Vandergiven alive?"

"Uh," she lifted her face to the ceiling. "Today's Saturday, and he didn't show up for work yesterday, so it was Thursday. I saw him at work on Thursday." She wailed again. "We had a date tonight!"

Leslie fished a business card from the pocket of her jacket. "Please give me a call if you think of anything." She rose from the chair and preceded Steve out of the room. She flashed a smile to see her case sitting by the front door. She wouldn't have to see Mr. Vandergiven again in order to retrieve it. Clutching the handle, she headed to her car.

"Think she knows anything?"

"No." Linn opened the trunk and tossed the case inside. "She isn't the brightest pebble on the beach, if you know what I mean, but I don't think she's a killer."

"Think Vandergiven died of natural causes?" Steve opened the driver side door for Linn, then jogged around to the passenger side.

"Do you?"

He shrugged. "Maybe. The lipstick throws a curve on

things, though. Doesn't it?"

"I'll check the case items tomorrow. Maybe, we'll get prints off the glass." She reached for the key and paused. "If Vandergiven was on a date, where's the other glass?"

"There wasn't one."

"Did you check the sink?"

Steve flushed. "No." He pulled a cell phone from his pocket. "I'll have the guys look for another glass."

Linn shook her head at the oft-times ineptitude of Upton Fall's police force. They really needed a new chief of police, someone who would be content with small-town crime. She was tired of filling in the position in a temporary way as well as her job as a detective and forensics. Budget cuts had left the department stretched way too thin. Since the death of Peter Lyman six months ago, crime was low in the small town. Just the way she liked it. She prayed Vandergiven had had a heart attack *after* his date.

The first responders, a man and a woman, the woman looking as if she should grace the cover of Cosmopolitan rather than deal with the dead or dying waited in the driveway for the go ahead to take the body.

"You can have him now," Linn said, marching past them.

~

The front of Vandergiven's house splashed in all its gaudy glory across her television screen. Reporters milled around on the front lawn, jostling for position. Linn frowned and turned down the volume. The newshounds would be bothering her tomorrow, wanting a statement. Especially the young Alan Rhoades, who seemed to be shadowing her way too much lately.

Her cell phone rang, its shrillness interrupting her thoughts, and she reached for the receiver. "Hello?"

"Hey, sweetheart."

Linn curled her legs beneath her, a smile spreading across her face. "Drew." His warm and throaty voice cut through the phone line, erasing the stress of the day.

"How was your day?"

"Got a call on a dead body. Found in his living room by, of all people, the secretary he was dating."

"Heart attack?" Drew's laugh rumbled through the line, and Linn giggled.

"Maybe. But the funny thing is, we found a lipstick print on the man's collarbone and on his little friend."

"A parting gift?"

"I don't know. How are things on your end?"

Drew was silent for a moment before answering. "We got the woman who abducted the baby from the hospital."

"And?" His voice told Linn there was more.

"We had to shoot her. It was her or the infant. She was dangling the little guy over a two-story balcony. The woman didn't survive."

"And the baby?"

"Safe at home with his parents. Luckily, she fell backward. A dangerous gamble, but one that needed to be made, or so the sniper says. Seems the woman was unable to have children of her own, so she decided to take someone else's. We've been trying to locate the husband, but he's disappeared."

"I'm sorry, Drew."

"Yeah." The silence stretched for several seconds before he spoke again. "Guess what?"

"We're engaged."

"Besides that."

"You're flying out this weekend." Linn ran a finger across the scar on her lip.

"No, sweetheart. I can't. There're some things I need to take care of here."

"You promised." Her heart plummeted to her stomach as his drawl deepened. "It's been two weeks. A long-distance engagement …"

"I don't think you'll mind too much when I tell you the

reason."

Linn sat up straighter. "Tell me."

"I've accepted the job as chief of police there in Upton Falls. Give me a week to tie things up here, and I won't be gone again."

Linn squealed. "For real?"

"For real." His laughter rolled through the phone. "How old are you?"

"Stop. I'm just excited." For the first time in her life, Linn felt free. Free enough to be who she was and not who those around her expected her to be. "Good. You can help me find the elusive love-interest of Mr. Vandergiven who apparently favors lipstick in the shade of Coral Sunset."

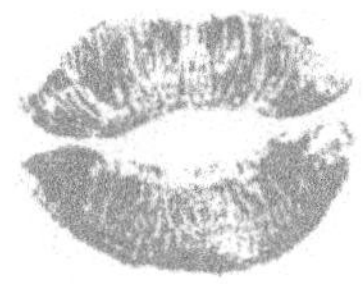

# Chapter Two

Linn handed the slide containing a smear of Coral lipstick to her associate. "Send this to DNA, would you? I'll be in my office." She peeled the gloves from her hands and tossed them in the nearby waste container. Placing her hands on her hips, she leaned back, popping her vertebrae.

Less than four hours of sleep just wasn't going to cut it. She wasn't sure which was worse, pounding the pavements as a small-town detective, or peering over microscopes, samples, and dead bodies as a forensic investigator. Not to mention the lack of Upton Falls having a chief of police. Lyman had killed a great man and a wonderful friend.

A slow smile spread across her face. That particular problem would be remedied soon enough. Her heart leapt at the thought of working with Drew every day, and her load lightened, putting a spring in her step as she headed down the hall and into her office.

Spread across her desk were copies of the photos taken at the Vandergiven home along with the notes in Steve's printing. Linn plopped in her chair and propped her feet on the desk after picking up the sheet of notepaper. She noted how tight and precise his letters were formed. Almost like a typewriter. Her partner was meticulous if nothing else.

The object of her musing appeared in her door, a mug in each hand. "Had your coffee yet?" Steve lifted one of the mugs to his lips.

"No. God bless you." Linn let her feet fall and reached for the offered mug.

Steve perched on the corner of her desk. "When are you going to stop burning the candle at both ends? You've been moving in hyper-speed since The Photographer case."

"We're short staffed." Linn blew into the steaming mug. "We ran blind on that case. I don't intend to let it happen on this one."

"I don't think your fiance would like to hear we were running blind, especially since he was leading the case."

"You know what I mean."

Steve rose from her desk. "Is that why you're turning to the forensic field? I thought you loved being a cop."

"I do. I did." Linn shrugged. "In a town like Upton Falls, I'll be doing a lot of both."

"You don't think Drew will try and keep a tight rein on you?" Steve walked to his own desk and sat down. "He almost lost you six months ago. I don't think he'll be taking any chances."

"Drew won't keep me from doing my job." Linn swiveled in her chair, transferring her attention to the photos spread across the desk blotter.

"Sure, he won't." Steve laughed.

Linn frowned. "Please tell me you've been doing more with your time than analyzing my upcoming marriage."

"Sure I have. I think I know where Vandergiven went before going home the other night."

"Where?" Linn pulled her head up.

"There's an upscale club in Upton Falls, where the rich often go after a tedious day at work. Vandergiven's secretary said he frequents the place quite a bit. It's very exclusive. You have to be a member, and the only women allowed are the ones who work there.”

“I’ve heard of it. He  won’t have picked up his mystery date at that club.” Linn pushed away from her desk. “Unless his killer is an exotic dancer.”

“Not necessarily.” Steve took another sip of his coffee. “Friday night just happens to be Ladies Night. The only night that women are permitted in.”

“Yeah? I can imagine the type of women who visit.”

“They’re very choosy about who they let in. The club prides itself on their clientele.”

Linn rose and grabbed a suit jacket from the back of her chair. After donning the navy blue blazer, she grabbed a photo of Vandergiven and slid it into the inside pocket. “Let’s go. I’ll drive.”

“Of course you will.” Steve set his mug on the desk and rose to join her. “I don’t think I’ve ever finished a cup of coffee for as long as we’ve been partners.”

“I’ll buy you another.”

“And you rarely let me drive.” Steve reached around her and pushed open the front door.

“You’re full of complaints this morning.”

“Must be the company.”

After an unseasonably warm winter, the spring’s temperatures were mild, and the two stepped out into a mid-eighty degree morning. Linn lifted her face toward the sun and closed her eyes, relishing the sun’s kiss on her skin.

She opened her eyes and smiled at Steve. “Maybe you should get a membership at this *exclusive* club. You might find a date.”

“Ha ha, but I can get a date on my own, thank you.” He opened the driver’s door for her before loping to the other side of Linn’s royal blue Mustang. Once inside the car, he spoke again. “Just because you’re getting married, doesn’t mean everyone else has to be in the same boat.”

"Just trying to help. You make marriage sound like a death sentence." Linn turned the key in the ignition and twisted to look behind them. Shifting the car into reverse, she backed out of the parking spot and roared down the street.

"I ought to give you a ticket for speeding." Steve clicked his seatbelt into place. "And put on your seatbelt."

Linn laughed and, keeping one hand on the wheel fumbled with her belt until it was secure around her. She rolled down her window, letting the wind rush past, pulling strands of her hair from its ponytail.

"Love has been good for you," Steve commented, a smile on his face. "You're lighter, more carefree."

"Not just love, Steve."

"I know. Love saved you from the pit of despair, pulling you out and lifting you up into radiance." He turned to look out his window.

"It's true. You notice the difference." She turned her eyes back to the road, weaving among the morning traffic as effortlessly as a porpoise navigated the ocean. She wished she could hear the seagulls and the pounding of the surf, but Upton Falls was several days away. Linn fully intended to solve this case and spend time at the beach, enjoying life with her new husband on a longer honeymoon than a few days in a mountain cabin, and not focusing entirely on corpses.

The Upton Falls Gentlemen's Club sat smack in the center of the downtown area, towering above boutiques, bars, and convenience stores. The white-painted concrete blinded the uncovered eye, and Linn grabbed her sunglasses from the glove compartment of her car. "Ritzy place." She slid from the Mustang and strode forward, leaving Steve to catch up.

"Bringing back memories?" Steve whispered.

"That's mean." Linn stared at the double-wooden doors inlaid with panels of shiny brass. "That was a long time ago, and I never danced in a place as fancy as this."

Grasping her elbow, Steve pushed the doors wide and steered her inside. They were met at once by the most muscular man Linn had ever seen. His biceps bulged against the seams of the black suit he wore. A shaved head shone despite the dim club lights. Steel grey eyes glared at them.

"May I help you?"

Steve flashed the man his badge. "We'd like to speak to the manager, please."

Without glancing at Linn, the man answered, "No ladies."

"I'm not a lady. I'm a police officer." Indignation rose in Linn, and her cheeks flushed.

Steve raised his eyebrows. "This is Detective McFarland, and I'm Detective Chavez. I repeat, we'd like to see the manager."

"That would be me." Still not looking at Linn, the man turned. "I'm Bruce Lyle. Follow me." He led them around skirted tables beside which were placed overstuffed tan sofas and armchairs. Unlit candle votives sat precisely in the center of each covered table. The dim lighting left the far corners unlit even during the day.

Bruce waved them into a small, wood-paneled office. He sat in the large leather chair behind the one desk, declining to offer them to sit.

Linn pulled Vandergiven's photo from her pocket and slid it across the polished desk top. "Ever seen this man?"

Bruce's gaze flicked to the photo. "We don't speak of our clientele. We have a very high standard of confidentiality."

"He's dead. How's that for confidentiality?" Linn picked up the photo and held it in front of the man's face. "Take another look."

The man sighed, his massive shoulders lifting, and let his eyes rest on the photograph in Linn's fingers. "That's

Vandergiven. He's here two or three times a week."

"Was he in here Friday evening?"

"Yes. He never misses Ladies Night."

Linn slid the photo back into her pocket. "Did he leave with anyone? Does he visit with a certain *lady* when he's here?"

"No, he likes them all. I can't remember if he left with anyone. We're very busy on Friday nights. A lot of classy broads come in here." Bruce folded his arms across his chest, straining his suit further. "I can't pay attention to every couple that strolls out the door."

"I'm sure." Linn handed him one of her business cards. "Give us a call if you remember anything." She dropped the card on the desk when he made no move to take it.

Bruce inclined his head toward Steve. "Does he speak, or do you do all the talking for both of you?"

"Know the saying 'good cop, bad cop'? I'm the bad cop, and I'm a real bitch on my best day." Linn spun on her heel. "Don't bother seeing us out. We know the way."

Once back behind the wheel of her car, Linn fumed, heat rising up her neck and into her cheeks. "Of all the pompous, chauvinistic…"

"You were pretty rude." Steve slid in beside her. "I do enjoy watching you get your dander up. You play the bad cop role well. Don't look now, but Mr. America is watching."

Linn whipped her head and locked gazes with Mr. Lyle, who stood with folded arms on the sidewalk in front of the club. The man's unblinking stare sent shivers down her spine, and she shuddered. Forcing her lips into a thin smile, she turned the key in the ignition, then pulled out of the club's parking lot.

"There's more there than meets the eye."

"You think?" Steve glanced over his shoulder.

"Why else would he follow us out?"

"Making sure we didn't snoop around."

"And what exactly was he afraid we'd find?" She cast a glance at her partner. "I really think you need to join that club."

"I doubt I'll be accepted now that you left such a favorable impression. It might be better to have Drew try."

Linn snorted. "That's not the type of place he'd enjoy. He prefers country music and sawdust on the floor. But, okay, I'll mention it to him." If he ever got around to actually moving to the same city in which his future wife lived.

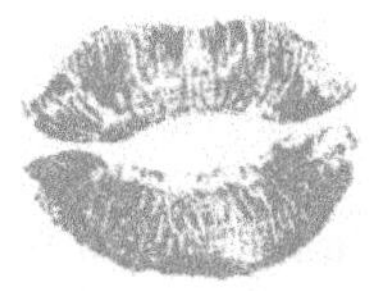

# Chapter Three

Linn wrinkled her face against the wetness and tried to squirm away only to find herself held in place by something clamped on each side of her. A weight sat on her chest, pressing the air from her lungs, and causing her to sink into the mattress. Her eyes snapped open, and in the split second before fully awakening, she opened her mouth to scream, then snapped it shut.

Drew leaned over her, his legs positioned on each side of her, keeping her in place, while a soft bundle of fur covered her face with slobbering kisses.

"Stop. Please." She fought harder to get herself free. "What is it?"

He rolled off her, scooping the squirming bundle in one hand. "A puppy. She's a gift."

"A puppy?" Linn propped herself up on one elbow. "Why'd you bring me a puppy?"

"Why not?" He leaned down, placing a kiss on her lips that could still send Linn's insides quivering.

Linn's eyes adjusted to the dim morning light. "You need a haircut." She ran her fingers through his ebony curls, then launched herself at him, shoving him back against the pillows. The blond wire-haired puppy yelped and dove beneath the covers. "I missed you. Tell me you're here to stay."

"I'm here to stay." Drew's strong arms tightened around her.

"Good, because I need help on this recent case. There's this club…"

He placed his index finger against her lips to quiet her. "Later. For now, I expect to be welcomed properly." Twisting his fingers in her hair, Drew pulled her face to his. His eyes smoldered with blue fire. He lifted Linn, then rolled over, placing himself on top of her. "Okay?"

"Okay." A slow smile spread across her face.

~

The yelping of the puppy in a crate beside the bed woke Linn, and she rolled over. She stared into Drew's sleeping face. One inky curl fell forward, covering an eye. Lashes too long to be wasted on a man lay on chiseled cheeks. Full lips open slightly and a square chin with just the hint of a cleft made him one of the handsomest men she'd ever seen. And he was all hers.

She smiled as his eyes opened, drowning her in their dark blue depths. The puppy's yelps increased in intensity.

"Good morning, again." Drew reached out and pulled her to him. "Someone wants to go out."

"You think?" The yelps vibrated against Linn's eardrums.

"Okay, I know you're bursting to tell me. What about this case?"

"Later." She planted a kiss on his lips and pulled away. "Over breakfast. Should I fix you an omelet?"

"Just coffee."

She pulled the sheet with her, wrapping it around her body in a toga style. "I get the shower first. Someone ought to take the puppy out."

"I will. Want me to get the coffee?"

"No, it's on a timer."

Linn dropped the sheet on the tiled floor of the bathroom and turned the faucet to the coolest temperature she could muster in the summer heat. She stepped beneath the cool spray and sighed, lifting her face to the water. She opened her eyes and squealed. "Drew!" Linn could just make out his shadowy form through the shower door.

He leaned against the jam of the bathroom door. "Puppy did her duty, and now I want to watch. It's kind of hard to see through the frosted glass, but my memory fills in the details."

"Stop it." She smiled to herself. If it took her a lifetime, she'd never get used to the admiration in his eyes when he looked at her or the warm softness of his voice when he spoke. She was definitely blessed. They'd pledged themselves to each other a few months ago. All they lacked was the formal piece of paper. Something she intended to remedy soon.

"Want me to scrub your back?"

"No. This shower isn't big enough for the two of us. Behave." She squirted a healthy dose of fruit fragranced shower gel onto a loofah sponge and proceeded to scrub her body.

"I've missed you, Linn."

"I've missed you." Her heart flip-flopped in her chest. The shower door slid open. "You're making me nervous." Her skin heated despite the cool water.

"Sorry." Drew folded his arms across his chest and leaned against the wall.

"No, you're not. Stop it." Linn's voice shook, and she rinsed off before reaching for the towel lying folded on the toilet seat. "How would you feel if I stared at you while you showered?"

He gave her a lopsided grin. "I wouldn't mind."

"No, I guess you wouldn't." She misjudged the step

from the shower and stubbed her toe along the door track, releasing a hiss as a stab of pain shot through that particular appendage. "The shower's all yours." She tried squeezing past him, only to find herself engulfed in his strong arms.

"My lady may pass for the price of but one kiss."

"Silly." Although standing at five feet eight inches in her bare feet, Linn had to tiptoe to plant a kiss on her husband's lips. "Price paid—gladly."

Drew swatted her bottom through the towel as she maneuvered her way around him. "Be out in a few."

Joy flooded through her as she pulled on her favorite navy pants then donned a white blouse. She picked up a comb from the dresser top and pulled it through her wet curls, catching a glimpse of herself in the mirror. She leaned closer, taking a better look at the scar on her lip. It still amazed her that Drew thought her beautiful. He even loved the wild, strawberry hair she could only tame by pulling it back into a bun or ponytail. Crazy, blind man that he was.

The doorbell's ringing pulled her from her thoughts, and she moved quickly to the front door. With a quick glance through the peephole, she opened the door to see her partner holding a bag of bagels from the local bakery. "Steve."

"Thought you might want a ride to work this morning." He stepped past her and stopped, his eyes widening as Drew stepped from the bedroom, dressed only in black pants and holding a squirming puppy. "Wayne."

"Hey, Chavez. You're just in time for coffee." Drew walked up and clapped the other man on the shoulder. "It's good to see you."

"Same here. Didn't know you were back."

"Got in early this morning." Drew planted a kiss on Linn's forehead. "Couldn't stay away."

Linn enjoyed the easy familiarity of the two men in her life. Six months ago they'd circled each other like junkyard dogs every time they got near each other. She still prayed daily that Steve would find a woman to love. Especially after she'd given her love to Drew instead of her partner.

The three of them headed into the kitchen. Drew opened the backdoor and gently pushed the puppy off the stair before the two men each took one of the wooden chairs around the table. Linn pulled down three porcelain coffee mugs as Steve unwrapped the sack of bagels.

"Good thing I bought a half dozen," he said.

"They smell yummy. Did you bring cream cheese?" Linn poured the coffee, fixing each mug the way they liked.

"You know I did. Have you told Drew anything about the case?" Steve accepted his mug with a smile of thanks.

"Not much." After handing Drew his mug, Linn took hers and plopped into an available chair.

"She tried," Drew laughed, his gaze lingering on Linn. His heavy-lidded glance made her knees weak. "But I brushed it off."

Steve's green-eyed gaze flicked between the two of them, settling on Linn long enough for a flush to rise to her cheeks. "I…see."

After taking a deep breath to steady herself, Linn cleared her throat. "Yesterday, Steve and I checked out a gentleman's club in Upton Falls that the victim had visited on the night he died. Friday night is Lady's Night at the club. The manager was rude, opinionated…"

"Stick to the facts." Steve raised his eyebrows.

She rolled her eyes. "The manager wasn't much help, but he *was* able to tell us that Mr. Vandergiven was there on Friday. Couldn't tell us whether he left with anyone though, and he couldn't tell us whether he spent more time with one woman than any others."

"Linn got to play bad cop, while I stood complacently by watching her rip into a man the size of King Kong."

Drew chuckled. "That's my girl." He took a sip from his mug, then set the mug on the table. "Not much to go on, is there?"

Linn shook her head. "I sent a smear of the lipstick to DNA, but, well, that's going to take a while. What about that friend of yours we used on The Photographer case? Do you think she could speed things along?"

"She's on vacation out of the country."

Linn shrugged. "Oh, well. Anyway, I want you to join this club. I've asked Steve, but he won't. He's the logical choice, but he's being obstinate."

"Why is Steve the logical choice? What's wrong with me?" Drew leaned back in his chair.

"You're getting married."

"So?"

"So." Linn glared. "It's not a place for any future husband of mine."

"I didn't think I should join since the manager already knows I'm a cop," Steve explained. "Especially, since I was there with Officer Godzilla. I'm sure she left quite an impression."

"He was a Neanderthal, and I wasn't that bad." Linn pouted, banging her mug on the table as she set it down.

"I see the reasoning here." Drew moved forward, letting his chair legs hit the floor with a thud. "Don't worry, sweetheart. I won't be bringing anyone home with me, and I'll only be looking with the eyes of a cop. Anyone in particular we're looking for?"

"A woman who wears coral-colored lipstick."

Drew shook his head. "I don't even know what that means. What is coral? Pink? Red?"

"A little of both." Linn pushed away from the table and rose. "Let me put the puppy away, and we'll go to the office. I'll show you."

"I have to get dressed." Drew stood. "Shall we meet you there, Chavez?"

Steve nodded. "Sure. I'll get together the little information we do have."

~

Drew slipped into his suit jacket, watching as Linn slicked mascara over her eyelashes. He smiled at the familiarity of her navy suit. "You know, you can wear something other than navy pants and a white blouse? The station doesn't really have a dress code. Not for detectives."

"I feel more comfortable. People take me more seriously if I look professional." She eyed his grey slacks and royal blue shirt with matching tie. "No dress code, huh?"

"Uh huh." He sat on the edge of the bed, sticking his fingers through the puppy's kennel. "You really should name her."

"Honey."

"Honey?"

"It suits her color." Linn turned away from the mirror. "What am I going to do with her, Drew? I really don't have time for a puppy."

"Train her. She's a lab mix. You can turn her into a K-9 cop or teach her to dig up dead bodies." Drew shrugged. "I found her wandering the street. I'm a sucker for kids and animals."

Linn wrapped her arms around his neck. "My big soft cowboy. Maybe I should take her to the office with us."

"Darn right." He loved the way she fit in his arms. Warm and soft. He thanked God for her. Every morning upon awakening and every night before falling asleep. "Come on. Let's go see what coral lipstick looks like."

"I'll drive."

Drew sighed and released her. "Once I get myself a truck, I'll drive."

"We'll see."

"Woman, you are the damndest thing I've ever seen." He ran his hands through his hair. "You make me feel as if you're my chauffeur."

Linn gave him a smile sure to melt his heart. "I'm your everything."

~

She watched as the men milled around the entrance to the 80s-style bar. Some had women with them, others didn't. Her hands ran down her body, caressing the curves she knew men desired and attracting the attention she craved. Her coral lips curved into a feline smile as one interesting prospect glanced in her direction.

Sauntering in tight jeans and three-inch stiletto heels, she brushed past him leaving a scent of musky perfume in her wake. She timed it just right so one finely sculpted arm brushed across his chest. She turned to squeeze past, her breasts skimming his chest. His slight intake of breath fueled her power, and she tossed him a glance over her shoulder, causing the silky cascade of her hair to sway.

As she'd planned, he followed, shoving aside other men who attempted to engage her in conversation.

"Hello, beautiful." His tone was slightly nasal beneath the handlebar mustache he wore, and she swallowed down her distaste, smiling instead.

"Hello, yourself," she purred.

"Got a name?"

"Yes."

He laughed, his eyes glazed from one too many martinis, and signaled the bartender. "I'm Bill."

"Don't bore me with names." She ran the sculpted fingernail of her index finger down his chin. "You can call me anything you want."

"I'll call you a dream, if you'll let me."

She pouted, her full lips pursed as she leaned closer to him. "I'm anything but a dream." More like a nightmare. This was going to be easier than she'd thought. No more leading the men to slaughter. From now on, she'd keep them and make them pay by serving her in whatever capacity she wanted.

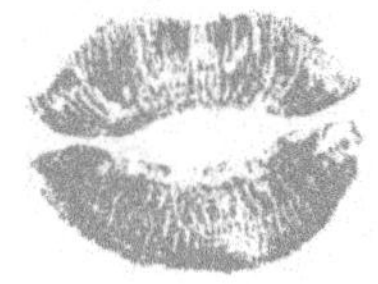

# Chapter Four

Ladies Night at the gentleman's club, and Linn had to leave her gun at home. The outfit she wore left little to the imagination, especially if she'd tried to hide a weapon. Should things get ugly, it would be up to Drew and Steve to take control. She was only there to scope things out and search for a woman wearing coral lipstick. Not that the particular color would signify the wearer as the murderer, but definitely as a person of interest.

The giant of a manager recognized her. She felt his glare as she traveled the room searching for a seat at the long bar. Steve had arrived with her and taken up residence in a booth. Already his stylish good looks attracted a crowd of eager beauties.

She perched on an empty stool at the bar and angled herself to get a clear view of the door. When Drew stepped inside, gorgeous in jeans, a blue button- up shirt, and his cowboy boots, with his hat in his hand, Linn could swear the room almost hushed. How did he get inside without wearing a suit? She smiled and crossed her legs, causing the tight leather skirt she wore to ride up a couple of inches.

She knew he'd seen. They'd played the game before; pretending they didn't know each other.

But, not this time. This time he needed to flirt with women other than his fiancée. Their game of pretend was serious now. How else would he draw out a possible predator? Linn didn't like it one bit. She turned to the bartender. "A cosmo, please."

Yes, she was working, but she wasn't officially on duty. A couple of drinks wouldn't hinder her capabilities if she needed to take someone down. Drink in hand, she swiveled back around…and glared.

Several scantily dressed beauties fluttered around Drew. When one woman, thick dark hair falling down her back like sensual chocolate sashayed up, she dismissed the other women with one wave of her elegant hand. Drew smiled down at the petite beauty and motioned to the bartender.

When he cast a quick glance at Linn, she lifted her chin and turned away. For a second. No way would she stop watching the female predator stalk her prey. Other than her days as an exotic dancer, a time in her life she wanted to forget, Linn never indulged in the game of sexual cat and mouse. The intricacies intrigued her, though. Too bad it had to be Drew playing the mouse.

She tore her attention away. Steve seemed to be fending off his own advances. A blonde and a redhead sat on each side of him. Steve's odd-colored eyes glittered. While Linn doubted he'd find a woman to love at a fancy gentlemen's club, she was happy to see that he enjoyed the women's attention.

For a while, he'd seemed focused on Linn as a romantic partner, angered when she chose Drew. He'd even been a person of interest in the Photographer case a few months ago. Linn may have been the only person in the state who'd believed him innocent from the very beginning.

She raised her glass in a toast in his direction. He

nodded and turned back to his company.

"Why is a beautiful woman such as yourself sitting here all alone?" Drew sidled up to the bar.

"No one has stepped up that I've been interested in." She left out the fact that she might as well have hung a "stay away" sign around her neck. Linn learned a long time ago that she could adopt a look that made men steer clear. She tossed her hair. "Until you, that is. What happened to the brunette?"

He shrugged and ordered a beer. "Not sure. We talked for a while about the usual flirtatious nonsense, then she moved on. Wait, she's approaching Steve. This club definitely attracts high class looking women."

"If you say so." Linn watched as the woman waved away the girls and sidled onto the booth under Steve's arm. "Looks like she plans on staying awhile. Did she seem suspicious at all?"

"No, just very confident."

"Did she ask you to leave with her?" Linn held her breath while holding her martini glass to her lips.

"No." He frowned. "Is that what happened to the vic?"

"Speculation." She downed the last of the drink and motioned for another. "I hate the bar scene no matter how much it's fancied up."

"Necessary in this case. Well, I'd best get back to setting myself up as bait."

Linn grabbed his arm before he left. "Be careful. Something feels...wrong."

"Murder is always wrong."

She shook her head. "It's more than that. I have a feeling this case will have more twists and turns than a roller coaster. I can't really explain it, only that you need to be careful."

"I will." He almost bent to kiss her, than straightened. "Almost forgot for a minute." He grinned and strolled away.

~

While appearing relaxed, Drew kept his gaze searching the room. The club had a good thing going with Lady's Night. Not only was it the only night of the month women were allowed entrance, but management was very choosy about whom they allowed in. Only the best dressed and the most beautiful gained access. Who knew Upton Falls, Arkansas, had so many gorgeous women? Of course, some could come from the neighboring towns, which would make solving this murder more difficult.

"Anything?" Steve bellied up to the bar, ordered a glass of white wine, then turned to face the milling hunters.

"Nothing. You?"

He shrugged. "There's a lot of hungry women, but none who seem like a killer. Of course, our lady probably won't look the part."

Drew's attention switched to the entrance. A petite woman with hair the color of a raven and eyes the color of whiskey made her way toward him and Steve. "I'll let you have this one." Drew grabbed his beer and made a quick getaway. The woman might look like she'd stepped off the pages of Vogue, but there was no mistaking the ravenous look in her eyes.

Finding an empty table, he sat in a chair that allowed him to see every entrance and sat back to watch Steve fend off the woman's advances. Not that Linn's partner seemed to be pushing the woman away. For the first time since he'd known the man, Steve seemed entranced.

Linn perched on the table next to Drew. "Act like you can't get over my beauty."

"Already there, sweetheart." Drew pulled her onto his lap. "You were blocking my view."

"Oh, Steve has a friend." Linn stood and sat in the chair next to him. "Have you had any takers?"

"Lots, but I've managed to avoid them. Until this flirty red head started to bother me." He pulled her close and kissed her long and hard. She tasted of something fruity.

She planted her palms on his chest and pushed him away. "I kind of like this game of cat and mouse."

"Brat." He grinned, then watched as the woman with Steve fingered his buttons. Things were getting hot and heavy very fast. "There's so much steam coming off those two, I'm about to dump a bucket of water on them."

"It would be nice if Steve found someone."

"I doubt he'll find anyone of any value in a bar, no matter how classy the place." He took a small sip of his beer. Ugh. In an attempt to make the drink last, it had gotten warm. "But, then again, he can't be working if he's got a leech attached to him."

"What if she's our killer? I could go rescue him, but then we might miss our chance."

She had a point. One that sent ice through his veins. He and Steve may have had their clashes over who would win Linn's heart, but Drew didn't want the man in the clutches of a murderer either. "Maybe you could go stand next to them like you're ordering a drink. See what you can hear."

"Got it." She sashayed to the bar, her slim hips causing the hem of her skirt to inch up her thighs.

Drew swallowed against the lump in his throat and shifted on the plush chair. Would Linn always send his blood pounding? He hoped so. He raised his hand for a barmaid to bring him a fresh beer. Maybe he should have asked for a bucket of ice for his lap while he was at it.

~

Linn squeezed next to Steve and ordered a bottle of sparkling water. Steve's new friend stood so close to him, little light made it between them.

"You can call me whatever you want. Who needs names?" She slipped her hand between the buttons on his shirt.

Linn wanted to gag. Seriously? That kind of talk was sexy? She gripped her glass of water and leaned against the bar, pretending as if she didn't care what was going on next to her.

"Do you want to get out of here?" The woman practically purred.

"Not yet." Steve pulled her hand free. "I'm with friends."

"I'm sure they can find their own way home." She pressed against him.

Linn had a name for her. She sipped her drink in order to keep her tongue occupied. The woman didn't seem like a killer, just a major slut. Oops, there went the name calling. She stepped sideways and bumped Steve, causing him to stumble into the woman with no name. "I'm sorry."

"Idiot." Miss No Name brushed at the spot of wine on her white dress. "If you can't be classy, you don't belong here." She glared at Linn over Steve's shoulder.

He put his arm around the woman's shoulders. "It was an accident. Why don't you go to the women's room and put some water on that. I'll be here when you return."

She gave him a simpering smile and strolled away. If her hips swung any harder, she'd break in half.

"Sorry, but you looked like you needed rescuing." Linn grinned.

"Not this time. Didn't you get a good look at her? Gorgeous." Steve set his empty glass on the bar.

"Someone has a crush." Linn wiggled her eyebrows.

"I might take her number. I'd like to see if she's as interesting without a drink."

"I haven't actually seen her take a drink." Linn glanced at the woman's full glass on the bar. "Are you sure she's tipsy?"

"She acts like she's more than tipsy. Have you and Drew had any luck?"

"No." She sighed. "He runs from every woman who looks twice at him, and I'm not approaching men because our suspect is female. I'm here to help where needed."

"Like running off the only woman I've expressed an interest in a long time." Steve fixed his light green eyes on her. "Don't I deserve a taste of what you and Drew have?"

"I'm sorry if I overstepped my boundaries. I'll leave. Here she comes." Linn marched to the other end of the bar but stayed within earshot.

"I'm glad you got rid of the third wheel," the woman cooed. She grabbed a napkin from the bar and asked for a pen. "Here's my number. I hope you call me. Otherwise," She tapped his chin. "I'll be here next week looking for you." She ground against him, then sauntered away.

"She's trouble," Linn muttered. Her partner deserved better.

"You're acting like my sister." Steve sidled up next to her. "I appreciate the gesture, but I'm a big boy. I can take care of myself. Don't you recognize her? She was one of the first responders at Vandergiven house."

"So? You can't find anyone of value in a bar."

"This is a nightclub." Steve ordered another drink.

Linn eyed him. "How many have you had? We're working."

He clenched his jaw. "Stop nagging me. I'll drink what I want and see who I want. In fact," he waved the paper in front of her. "I'll be calling, whoever she is, when I get home."

"Fine by me." Linn stormed away. Fool. All she wanted to do was make sure he found someone to make him happy.

~

She watched from the shadows as the skinny redhead talked with the handsome olive-skinned man at her side. After a few words, her target stormed away. Queen Coral, as she preferred to be called, smiled and followed.

The man headed to the men's room. Perfect. She'd wait outside and approach him when he exited. When a taller, more handsome man came up, she stepped into a closet and closed the door, leaving an inch to peer out.

Several minutes later, the men came out together, the shorter one leaning on the tall one. She scowled, her chance gone. No matter. She'd see him again. No man could resist her for long.

She stepped out of the closet and watched as the two men left, the redhead trailing behind. Interesting. The three seemed to be friends. Maybe a little investigating needed to be done before the Queen took out the target. Still, her hunger needed satisfying.

She scanned the room, focusing on an unsteady young man with the body of a god. He guffawed with some other men before stumbling out the front entrance. Coral lifted her chin and pursued him.

"Hey, handsome. Don't tell me you're leaving alone."

"Not anymore." The man leaned against a Ford truck and fumbled with his zipper. "We have a few minutes before my friends come out."

She sidled closer. "Not here. I have a car. I can take you home afterward."

"I don't know. They'll be looking for me. Tonight's my twenty-first birthday."

"Well, I have a present I know you'll like." His birthday? It couldn't be more perfect. How fascinating that his birth and death should coincide on the same day, unless he pleased her. She took his tie in her fist and led him toward her Porsche like a lamb to the slaughter.

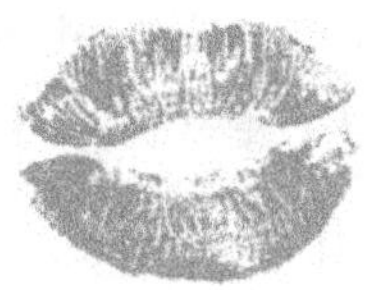

# Chapter Five

Steve dialed the number on the slip of paper in his hand. It was way past time for him to get over Linn. She was engaged to Drew. Their last assignment had almost gotten them both killed. He didn't want to die without having love in his life. If he couldn't have Linn, there might be someone else out there for him.

"Hello?" The woman's husky voice heated his blood.

"This is Steve Chavez. We met at the club last night?"

"Yes, I remember you." The sound of fabric drifted through the phone. The thought that he might have woken her, that she might not be clothed, made his pulse race. "What can I do for you, Steve?"

"I was wondering if you were free for dinner tonight? I know this great seafood place on the lake."

"I know of it." She chuckled, the sound deep and throaty. "I'm free. What if I meet you there at seven? I trust you remember what I look like?"

"Of course." How could he forget? Long and leggy with dark hair that fell in a waterfall past her shoulders. Pouting lips and bedroom eyes. If nothing worked out for them romance-wise, it wouldn't hurt him to have a dalliance. It had been a long time.

He swung his legs over the side of the bed. Not that he was one of those men who cheapened women by looking at them as sex objects, but if it was the right woman, and she was willing, he wasn't above wining, dining, and bedding.

A cold shower didn't erase the grin from his face by the time he waltzed into work. Linn glanced up with a puzzled frown, then returned to the papers on her desk.

"I'm not going to ask," she said.

"I'm not going to tell you." He handed her a Styrofoam cup of coffee and perched on the corner of her desk. "Where's the boss?"

"Pretending to be single and toget information out of the manager of the gentleman's club. Thanks." She took the coffee and breathed deep.

"Better him than me."

"Hmm." She stared into her cup. "Let's go over the women at the club who might be a possible suspect. We have to start somewhere. What about the woman with the long dark hair. Did you get her name?"

"Which one?" There had been two dark-haired beauties paying him attention.

"Both."

"Didn't catch either name. Not the blond, either. It seems as if the women don't give those out freely." Strange. He'd seen slips of paper trading hands, had one in his pocket, but hadn't heard any names.

"High-priced call girls?"

He shrugged. "Maybe. We could look into it at least." He turned to his computer and came up with three top escort services. After printing out the list, he handed it to Linn. "Ready?"

She nodded. "We have to start somewhere. I'll let Drew know we're going. He's busy settling in. If we find something of interest, he can meet us."

"Yeah, the chief-of-police sits mainly behind a desk." Steve shuddered. "Not the job for me."

Linn laughed. "Me neither. Let's see how long it takes Drew to figure out he hates it."

"I give him three months." Steve grabbed his suit jacket and followed Linn to her new jeep. One of these days, she was going to have to let him drive.

~

It would take everything in her power not to arrest the woman sitting in front of her. "Escort services are not a front for prostitution," the woman said. "The women are paid to be companions. To attend functions with gentlemen. If they choose to have a fling, that is up to them."

"As long as they aren't being paid for it," Linn said, rolling her eyes. "Look, Ms. Armstrong, we both know what your girls do for money. Now, answer my question, or I will haul you to jail."

The woman gave a long-suffering sigh. "Very well. No, I do not believe any of my girls are capable of murder." She slid an album across her desk. "Here are their photographs and aliases."

Linn placed the book between her and Steve and flipped through the pages. Two women wore what could be considered a coral-colored lipstick. She pointed them out. "We need the real names of these two women." Of course, the others could wear that shade, but it gave them someone to start with. "I also want the names of anyone else who wears this shade of lipstick."

Ms. Armstrong rolled her eyes and wrote on a post-it note. "This goes against our rules."

"Thank you for your time." Linn stood and marched out of the office.

"Why don't you try being a little nicer once in a while?" Steve shook his head. "Or let me do the talking?"

"My way is effective." She cut him a sideways glance.

He shrugged. "True, but you don't make many friends."

"I'm not out to make friends." She pressed the button on her car fob and unlocked the doors. "Let's visit the other two bordellos and then the people of interest."

"They aren't bordellos." He grinned.

"Same thing in my opinion."

She climbed into the driver's seat and headed to Little Rock.

The second location was as far from the cement-and-glass building of the first as it could be. A small space in a strip mall, appropriately titled "Lonely Gentlemen." A single glass door jingled as Linn pushed it open.

A pretty redhead who couldn't be more than eighteen greeted them with a smile which quickly faded when they flashed their badges.

"We'd like to speak to the person in charge," Linn said.

"I'll get him."

Linn glanced at Steve. "Him?"

"Maybe this isn't the type of escort service we're looking for."

"Or maybe we've been assuming the killer is female."

"May I help you?" A small, thin man in an expensive suit and turquoise shirt headed their way. "I'm Markus Kline." He held out his hand.

"Detective McFarland." Linn returned his shake. "This is Detective Chavez. May we speak to you in your office… please?" She glanced at Steve and raised an eyebrow.

He smiled and nodded.

In a small office, stylishly decorated in blues and greys, Mr. Kline waved them to their seats. "Have I done something wrong?"

"Not unless you wear coral lipstick?" Linn pierced him with her gaze.

"I am not a cross-dresser, ma'am. None of my…boys are."

"None of them dress as women when working?"

"No. I screen my employees very carefully. They are

disease-free, handsome, and well-groomed. While this is a homosexual business, I do not allow cross-dressing. That is grounds for immediate dismissal." He folded his hands on the desktop. "Our clients deserve to know what they're getting."

"Thank you for your time. We're sorry to bother you." Linn never sat. She'd known they were in the wrong place from the moment she met the man. While obviously gay, he was not flamboyant in any way. Not to say that one of his employees wouldn't put on lipstick to thrwart the police, but it didn't ring right to her.

"I hope you find who you are looking for."

"I think we're wasting our time," Linn said, back in her jeep. "I think keeping our eye on the gentleman's club is a better bet."

"I do, too, but we can't rule anything out. On to the third place?"

"Yeah." She sighed and turned the key in the ignition.

The third location was housed out of a massage parlor. Sometimes the world's filth weighed on Linn's shoulders. She would need a shower when she got home.

The receptionist, Amanda Reynolds, from the name on her deskplate, wore the exact shade of lipstick as their perp. "Miss Reynolds, where were you two nights ago?"

She paled and pushed back in her chair. "At the movies." She fished in her purse and pulled out a ticket. "First showing." She handed the stub to Linn.

"Do you frequent the gentleman's club on Friday nights?"

"The what?" She frowned.

"Nevermind. May we speak with the person in charge, please?" Miss Reynolds wasn't the killer. It wasn't going to be an easy case.

"Mrs. Wyatt is out of town, but here is her cell phone number." The receptionist handed over a business card. "She returns next week."

"Thank you." Another dead end.

"Let's grab lunch and then visit the individuals," she told Steve as they stepped back outside.

Both of their phones dinged.

Linn checked the face. "We've got a homicide." She messaged back that they were on their way. Ten minutes from where they were. "Drew said there is a lipstick print on the man's collarbone."

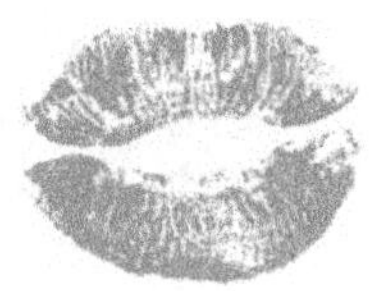

# Chapter Six

Linn squatted next to the body of a man in his twenties and took a swab of the coral-colored lipstick on his neck. Female serial killers were rare, but they did pop up once in a while. She had a horrible feeling they may be dealing with one.

"Have the lab compare this to the one from Vandergiven." She handed the swab to Steve, who dropped it into a bag. "We need to find out if this man was at the club."

"He was." Another young man, his eyes red-rimmed, stepped forward. "We went together. It was his birthday. When we stepped out into the parking lot, Bryan was gone."

Planting her hands on her thighs, Linn pushed to her feet. "You didn't see whom he left with?"

The man shook his head.

"What's his last name?"

"Givens." He swiped a hand across his eyes.

"How did you know where to find him?"

"We have GPS on each other's phones. I knew the

proximity and kept looking until I found…him."

Steve fished in the dead man's pockets and pulled out a cell phone. "We should be able to find out where he was last night."

"I already know. He was there." He pointed at a seedy motel across the street from the vacant lot. "At least, that's what the GPS said. I didn't go looking for him last night because he said he was with a woman. When he didn't answer this morning, I tried calling because we were going to be late for work. He didn't answer, so I came over to drag his ass out of bed."

"What's your name, son?" Steve pulled a notepad from his pocket.

"Seth Daily."

"You've been a big help. Would you mind going over to that officer to give your statement?"

He nodded and shuffled away, giving one last, sad look at his friend.

"Paramedics are here." Linn motioned toward the approaching ambulance.

A gorgeous woman with dark hair tied back in a ponytail approached them. No makeup, smooth skin, a petite curvy figure…Linn felt like a clumsy giraffe next to her. As the woman moved closer, she recognized her from the club.

Apparently, so did Steve, considering the grin on his face. "So we meet again."

The woman laughed. "I hope our date won't run late." She flicked a glance at Linn, then offered her hand. "Meaghan Larson."

"Detective McFarland." Linn returned her shake, then glanced at Steve, raising her eyebrows. So her partner had a date.

With one last smile at Steve, Meaghan moved to the body. The medical examiner pronounced the man dead, and Meaghan and her partner loaded the body onto a gurney.

"A date, huh?" Linn said, packing up her equipment.

"Don't start."

"Start what? I think it's wonderful. She's quite a looker. I never figured you for the type to pick up a woman at a bar."

"Club, not bar."

Drew's truck pulled into the lot. He climbed out and hurried toward them. "Sorry I'm late. Unfortunately, there's a lot of paperwork to go with my job. What did I miss?"

"Steve has a date." Linne grinned. "With a beautiful paramedic."

"Way to go, man." Drew clapped him on the shoulder.

"You two need to grow up." Steve shook his head and headed for the jeep.

"Let's go for coffee and you can fill me in," Drew said.

"Sounds wonderful." She tossed Steve the keys to her jeep, promising to meet him back at the station.

Ten minutes later, she sat across from Drew at a small round table and sipped a frozen mocha drink. "We wasted our morning visiting escort services. I think we have a serial killer on our hands."

Drew nodded. "It's starting to look that way. The news, thankfully, left out the information on the perpetrator's lipstick. For two men to die with lip prints on their skin isn't a coincidence or a copy cat."

At least this killer wasn't after Linn. She'd almost been killed six months ago by a deranged man obsessed with her. Not to mention Steve had been taken hostage and thrown into a pit. "All we have to go on is the lipstick."

"Maybe DNA will tell us something."

"More likely, the prints won't be in the system, nor will there be a record of DNA." She twirled her cup on the table.

"We caught The Photographer, we'll catch this person, too." He reached across the table and placed his hand on hers. "We now know we can focus our efforts on women attending the club on Friday nights."

"Unless Givens was picked up in the parking lot by someone who hadn't been inside. This woman, if it is a woman, could have been lying in wait."

"This coming Friday, I'll keep an eye on the parking lot. You and Steve can case the inside. I cannot believe the place doesn't have security cameras. Violation of privacy, my hat."

"Steve and I are still going to visit the names on our list." Linn stood. "Maybe the women cruise the club looking for clients."

"It's a good idea." With his hand on the small of her back, Drew escorted her to his truck. "It's back to paperwork for me. I can honestly say I prefer the streets."

"Steve gives you three months before you quit."

"So, it's a challenge?"

The gleam in his eye told her he would at least last three months and a week. She grinned. "I suppose it is."

~

"Don't give me the third degree on…Meaghan," Steve said as they pulled in front of the first address.

"What's the matter? You didn't know her name?"

There was no way in hell he was going to tell her that he hadn't known the name until an hour ago. "Of course I did. We spoke on the phone last night." They exited the jeep and approached the house. Steve pressed the doorbell. "No more questions."

"No promises."

It took three rings before someone answered the door. A lovely blonde in short shorts and a sports bra opened the door. In one hand, she clutched a water bottle. "What's the hurry? You'd better not be selling anything."

Linn flashed her badge. "We'd like to ask you a few questions."

Her eyes widened. "Am I in trouble? Look, my job is

completely legit—"

"May we come in?" Steve motioned toward the door.

"Sure." She moved back, allowing them entrance. "Have a seat. Excuse the mess."

Steve, a minimalist and clean freak cringed at the stack of laundry on the sofa, magazines on the coffee table, and a very large mixed-breed dog curled up on the easy chair. "I'll stand," he muttered.

"Suit yourself," Linn said, shoving aside the laundry. "Miss…Smith…is that your real name?"

"Yes." The woman smiled. "I go by Amber Gold with my clients."

"Where were you Friday night?"

"At a charity function. Most of my clients pay well to have a woman like me on their arm."

"Do you wear the lipstick shade Coral Sunset?"

"Of course. It's the newest shade. Most of the stores can't keep it stocked."

Steve sighed. If she was right, their job just got a lot harder. "Do you attend the gentleman's club on Friday nights in Upton Falls?"

"Not very often. I'm usually working. When I'm not, I patrol the club and hand out business cards."

"What about the other women you work with?" Steve took notes on their conversation.

"I've seen a couple now and then." She set the water bottle on top of the stack of magazines, not caring that the sweating bottle left a wet ring.

Steve shuddered. "I think we have all we need for now." He handed her his card. "Please call if you think of anything else."

"But what are you looking for? If I knew, it might help."

"We're looking for a killer, Miss Smith."

She gasped and clutched his card.

"We'll see ourselves out." Linn stood and opened the

front door. "Please don't leave town."

Steve followed her to the jeep. "How can such a nice girl sell herself the way she does?"

"Maybe she's legit in that she doesn't take money for services provided, if you know what I mean."

"Perhaps." He climbed into the passenger seat. "The next name is a man."

"My gut tells me the killer is a woman, so let's skip that one."

"Then, we have an hour drive ahead of us."

"Let's grab wraps from Subway first. I'm starving."

"You're always hungry. I have no idea how you stay so thin."

"Good metabolism." She grinned and took the next exit from the highway. Once they had their lunch in hand, they headed south.

The next person on their list lived in a third-floor apartment. They tromped upstairs on the outside of the building and knocked. From the tousled look of the pretty redhead, they'd either woken her or she was working early.

"Can I help you?" She yawned, revealing straight white teeth.

They flashed their badges and she let them inside. A toddler with hair the same shade as the woman's played with blocks on the floor. "We can talk here," she said. "My son is deaf."

Steve got right to the point, asking her where she was on Friday, if she attended the gentleman's club, and if she wore Coral Sunset. He stared, pencil poised over his notepad and Linn squatted and signed words to the little boy.

"Coral Sunset? Not likely. That color does not go with my skin tone. I don't frequent the gentleman's club. My job keeps me away from my kid enough without me going out on my own." She smiled in her son's direction.

"What about the other ladies you work with?"

She shrugged. "No idea. We rarely see each other."

Linn stood. "Thank you for your time. Your son is a joy."

"He's my angel." She showed them to the door. "Sorry I couldn't be more help."

Back outside, Steve sighed and glanced at their list. "One more name. Violet Lilly." Where did these people make up their name? "It's close."

"Good. Because we're spinning our wheels."

Steve understood her frustration. They needed a clue. Several of them, in fact, to solve this case before someone else died.

Violet lived in a duplex in a shabby part of town. The dark-haired beauty glared once they showed their badges. Her sharp-blue gaze clashed with Steve's. "You look like one of those fellas that dine and wine a gal and then dump her."

Was she referring to her clients? Surely she didn't expect them to have more than a paid relationship with her. He rattled off the same questions they'd asked the others.

"Of course I go to the club. Where else am I going to find a husband? At work? I wouldn't marry one of those old geezers for anything. I dress pretty, smile, take their money, and come back to this dump."

"The lipstick?"

She grabbed a tube from a side table. "My favorite color."

Steve added her name to their list of suspects. Hers was the only name listed. She had a motive because she obviously disliked men. She frequented the club. She owned the lipstick. Not a lot to go on, but it was a start. He handed her his business card. "Please call us if you think of anything important."

"Not likely." She tossed the card on the table and showed them out.

"You should have let me do the talking," Linn said

once they were back in the jeep. "That girl ate you for lunch."

"Some people don't like cops."

"Or men."

"You used to be that way." He cut her a sideways glance, remembering the story she'd told of her rape while she was an exotic dancer. "We don't know what causes Miss Lilly to be the way she is."

"You're right. And women like her…have been known to kill."

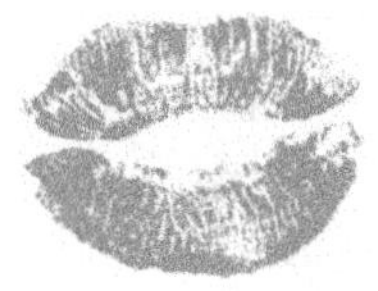

# Chapter Seven

Steve adjusted his tie, using his reflection in the restaurant's glass door. Satisfied with his appearance, he pushed open the door and stepped into the romantic ambiance. "Reservation for Chavez," he told the hostess.

"Right this way, sir." The woman, dressed in a black-and-white, tuxedo-style suit, led him to a table near the window.

Outside, a fountain bubbled from the urn of a plaster girl. Koi swam in the water of the basin, lazily moving between water lilies and other water plants. A white tablecloth adorned the table, a candle flickered in the center, and napkin-wrapped silverware waited to be used.

The atmosphere made the restaurant Steve's favorite place to eat. He had once tried envisioning Linn across the table from him, but Drew's arrival had squelched that particular dream. While he would always have feelings for his partner, it was time for Steve to move on. He glanced up and smiled as Meaghan strolled his way.

Gorgeous in a black dress that skimmed her curves and stopped a couple of inches above her knee, she drew the attention of male and females alike as she made her way to their table. Steve stood and pulled out her chair. "Hello."

"Hello." Her smile sent heat through his extremities. Her bedroom eyes peered up through thick lashes. She definitely knew how to use her beauty.

"So, you're a detective."

Steve raised an eyebrow. "And you're a paramedic. New to the area?"

"I am. I worked in Las Vegas for a while, but tired quickly of that scene." She leaned forward, showing just enough cleavage not to be vulgar. "I like the small town life."

"So do I. Things are quiet…most of the time." He handed her a menu.

"Until Queen Coral struck." Her lips twitched. "That's what the papers are calling her."

Steve sighed, wondering who had leaked the information on the lipstick. "That's too kind of a name for this killer."

She shrugged one shoulder. "Take one down, another comes along. It's the way of our ugly world." Opening the menu, she peered over the top. "Even in Upton Falls such cases could sour a man."

"Hasn't happened to me." Yet. The Photographer case had almost killed him. He hadn't known about an identical twin brother fixated on him and his partner. Not until it was almost too late. Crazed, with a facial deformity, his brother had lived his whole life jealous of the one who got away. Steve. It was a miracle he still believed in happy endings.

"I hope it never does. I'll take the lobster salad, please." She folded her menu and handed it to the waitress.

"Filet, nine ounces, medium rare with side salad and rice pilaf." Steve leaned against the back of the booth. "How does one flirt with a woman such as yourself? Should I tell you how beautiful you are? Ask why a woman such as yourself works as a paramedic and often sees very unpretty scenes?"

She laughed, the sound like music turned on low, soft and husky. "You seem to be doing just fine. As for my job, I love it. Yes, I run across the bad, but when we can save someone, it's worth it. I'm sure that's why you're a detective."

"I do my job to put the bad guys away." Keeping his gaze on hers, he asked, "why would someone like you frequent the club?"

"It's a better class of men than a bar." She straightened as their food was brought in front of them. "Why were you there?"

He grinned. "I heard it was Ladies Night."

"And stumbled across me." She twined her fingers with his.

~

Linn perched on the edge of Drew's desk. "Are you almost finished?"

He ran a hand through his hair and shook his head. "What a nightmare. Who kept up with the reports after Mad Dog died?"

"No one. Can't you tell?" She grinned. "Let's go home. I miss you. I'll even go country line dancing if it will get you out of that chair."

"Tempting, but I've got to get caught up. Why don't you go out and grab some takeout? We can at least eat together."

She groaned and grabbed her keys. "Chinese?"

He mumbled in the affirmative.

At first, she'd been ecstatic about his taking the job. Now, she hated it. She wanted him pounding the pavement with her, working on solving a case with little to no leads. Oh, well. She'd grab the food and work a caseboard for her and Steve to study in the morning. She couldn't just sit and watch Drew work.

With an order of fried rice, egg drop soup, and Kung

Pao chicken in hand, she stepped through a falling drizzle to her jeep. As she set the food on the passenger seat, a man stumbled down the sidewalk in silk boxer shorts. Checking to make sure the safety was off her holstered weapon, she closed the door to the jeep and followed him.

"Sir?"

The man leaned against the side of a building. "Help me."

"I will. Put your hands where I can see them, please."

He slid down the wall, raw marks around his wrists and ankles. Burns covered his chest.

Linn grabbed her radio from her belt and called for an ambulance. "What happened to you?"

"Abducted. Tortured. Three weeks ago."

"By whom?" She hadn't heard of any missing persons.

"A woman. She wore a mask when she came."

"What's your name?"

"Bill Nelson. I'm an accountant from Atlanta. No family. Not due back to work until next week. Do you have water?"

Which explained why no missing-persons report existed. "Stay there. Do not move." She dashed to the jeep and pulled a bottle of water from the carton she kept in the back. When she returned, she twisted off the lid and gave it to the man as an ambulance screamed to a halt beside them.

She stepped to the side and let the paramedics load him into the ambulance. Supper was going to have to wait. After letting Drew know what was happening and calling Steve who was not happy to be interrupted on his date, she followed the ambulance to the hospital.

"You don't have to come," she told her partner. "I only called to let you know. I can fill you in in the morning."

"Thank you." Click.

Good grief. She grinned, happy that he was enjoying himself, and put her siren on the top of the jeep.

At the hospital, she followed the gurney into a curtained

alcove and waited outside while a doctor examined the man. Once she'd been given the all clear to question him, she pulled a chair next to the bed.

"Do you feel like talking, Mr. Nelson?"

He nodded. "I'm glad to be out of there."

"Start at the beginning with where you were taken." She settled her gaze on his face.

"I was at a bar relaxing after a day of selling pharmaceuticals. I'm a rep. I stepped outside to have a smoke. It was dark. A blond woman approached me. We spoke and I went with her. She must have drugged me because I woke up in a basement, tied me to a chair. She tortured me, raped me…" he swiped a hand across his face. "I've never heard of that happening to a man."

"It happens." She studied the handsome man in front of her. He could very well be a cover model with his chiseled body, dark eyes and hair a shade lighter. "You never saw her face?"

"Not clearly. She spoke softly, like a hushed whisper."

"What color of lipstick did she wear?"

"A peachy rose color."

"How did you get away?"

He closed his eyes. "She was usually very careful. For days, I'd been working on my ties, finally cutting through them. I escaped through the basement window."

"Do you know the location?"

"An abandoned apartment building."

"You're a lucky man, Mr. Nelson. She killed the other men she took." She set a business card on the bedside table. "If you think of anything that will help us catch her, please give me a call."

"You can count on it. She needs to be put away. What she did to me was despicable." He pressed a button on the bed controls and lay down.

Linn drove back to the precinct and microwaved the cold Chinese takeout. Grabbing some paper plates from the lounge, she headed to where Drew still sat at his desk. After serving up the food, she settled into a chair across from him.

"Queen Coral abducted the man I found wandering the streets. He escaped. Doesn't know anything to help us other than the fact she wore the shade of lipstick we're looking for." She used chopsticks to grab a piece of chicken. "He's pretty out of it. Doesn't know the location of the building where he was held. The bar is the same as where we found the last victim."

"This is not going to be an easy case. One where Steve and I may have to step out as targets."

"You're going to leave your desk?" She grinned.

He crossed his arms and leaned back in his chair. "I've the looks to be a boy toy if a woman wants one." He winked.

"She kills the men she takes, Drew." Linn shuddered.

"I'd like to think I'm smart enough to not allow that to happen. Those men weren't expecting anything other than a one-night stand. I will be. Besides, I really miss undercover work."

She preferred him safely behind a desk. Drew tended to take chances. Ones that might leave her alone and grieving.

~

Queen Coral. She loved that name!

She unlocked the door to the basement. "Hello, darling."

Rounding the corner at the bottom of the steep stairs, she cursed. The man was gone. His chair empty except for the silk bindings she'd used to hold him. She caught sight of the broken basement window and threw the closest thing at hand. A lantern.

It shattered, spilling oil across the floor. Very well. She'd find a new place and a new toy to keep there. She took a match from the box on a table and tossed it onto the oil. With one last glance, she headed up the stairs and into the night air.

A good night ruined. The latest man she'd had her eye on would be missed too much should he disappear. The others…they were merely there to feed her hunger. It was getting more and more difficult. The hunt took her further out of town. To frequent the same bars too often would be futile and result in her capture. She wasn't ready.

There were too many men who had to pay for what had been done to her.

Anger rolled through her, coming off in waves she could see. A red aura glowed from her body. Coral that matched the lipstick she wore.

She drove to the nearest seedy bar. A place normally below her standards. She needed to kill or lose her mind.

She sat in the parking lot, scoping out the men coming and going. Most were old or overweight, a couple were young and good-looking.

There. A guy, little more than kid really, wearing a letter jacket from Arkansas State.

Just as she started to get out of the car, a girl grabbed his arm and pulled him toward a truck.

Queen Coral sighed and settled back to wait. It wouldn't be too long before the bar closed, and a bug would get entangled in her web. She spent the time thinking of how she would kill him and how she would leave her mark. When she tired of that, she planned her next move on finding a toy to keep. She was much pickier when it came to that.

She rubbed her hands together. Oh, yes, this was the fun part.

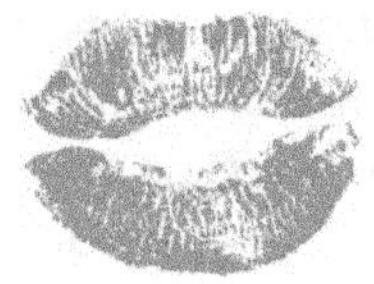

# Chapter Eight

The man in the chair stirred, then groaned. His eyes flickered.

"Oh, good, you're waking up." Coral pulled on a clear mask that distorted her features and settled the platinum-blond wig into place. "I was getting rather bored."

"Where am I?"

"Don't worry about that." She pulled up a chair and sat across from him. "Men are pigs, did you know?"

He frowned and glanced down. "Where are my clothes? I'm into some kinky stuff once in a while, but you beat everything I've ever seen."

"Good," she smiled. "I want you to remember me."

He gave a lopsided grin, revealing slightly crooked bottom teeth. "So, what's first?"

"My, aren't we eager." That would change soon enough. Once the pain started, he would realize she wasn't playing. Sure, he was there to satisfy her never-ending cravings, but he was also there to heal the pain she'd endured in the past at the hands of men she trusted.

She grabbed a thin wire and heated it over a burning

candle. "Let's get started, shall we? I have a club to get to." She wrapped the hot wire around his neck and laughed as he screamed.

~

Linn sat on a barstool, legs crossed and tried to look disinterested in the men's appraising glances sent her way. In actuality, she fumed at the way a pretty redhead draped herself across Drew. Undercover work was the pits!

Drew tossed her a wink over Redhead's shoulder, then transferred his attention back to the chattering vixen. When she placed a hand on his chest, Linn wanted to shoot her.

"Relax." Steve perched on the stool next to her. "Drew isn't interested in anyone but you."

"Right, but that woman is *clearly* interested in him. Where's Meaghan?" Steve hadn't left his new friend's side since she arrived an hour ago.

"Restroom." He smiled. "I may have found the one, Linn. She's smart, beautiful, and likes to have a good time."

"I'm happy for you. I really am." She smiled as Meaghan glided—there was no other word for the way the woman walked—to them.

"Evening, det…oops, Linn, right?"

"Yes." Linn returned her smile but kept her eyes on Drew.

"Would you like me to get rid of the slut, so you can introduce yourself to the cowboy?"

Steve jerked.

Linn's eyes widened. "Uh, sure." She turned to her partner as Meaghan moved away. "Didn't expect that type of language to come out of such a classy-looking woman."

"She's full of surprises." He raised a glass of white wine to his lips. "She knows we're working together, but I haven't told her about Drew. I figure the least amount of people who know, the better. Especially with him working undercover."

"I agree. You can tell her later." She slid off the stool and headed Drew's way as the frowning redhead stormed off. "Thanks," she told Meaghan, sliding into the booth next to the man she loved. "Hello, handsome."

"You're the most gorgeous woman I've seen here tonight."

Meaghan's eyes flashed. "I'll just leave you two alone." With a toss of her head, she returned to Steve.

"That's an odd woman," Linn said, "but Steve is infatuated with her. I don't think she liked the idea you thought me prettier."

"You're always the most beautiful, at least to me." Drew motioned around the room. "Seems plenty of other men share the same sentiment. Have you learned anything?"

"Just that I don't like you being undercover this way." She shrugged. "We're watching all the women, having them sign in at the door. Same with the men. The manager agreed to say it was a new policy. Hopefully, this way, if someone disappears, and their name is on the list, we have suspects to start with. It's a long shot, but it's all we've got."

"Toward closing time, I'm going to have to pretend to be drunk and hang around outside."

"I don't like it. I'll find a place to hide."

"No, you'll stay here. If you're spotted, you'll blow my cover."

She would find a way to keep him in her sights. There was no way she was going to allow him to become Queen Coral's next victim. Maybe she could convince Steve to let his girl go early and playact with her. If they were lucky, they'd catch the killer that evening.

"I suppose I shouldn't monopolize your time," she said, motioning to the bartender. "But I don't like all the women coming around either."

"Scoot a little closer." He put his arm across the back of

the bench. "We can pretend to be drunk and only have eyes for each other."

"Sounds like fun." She scooted closer and caressed his cheek. "You need to shave."

"What? You don't like the scruffy look? It seems to be quite popular with the ladies."

"Even more of a reason to shave."

He pulled her close for a rough kiss. "Stop being jealous. I love you."

"Ditto." She ran her fingers through hair always in need of a cut. Still, the loose curls and facial scruff were very sexy. Not to mention the way he could look at you with half-closed blue eyes. No wonder most of the women in the club shot daggers her way.

Drew glanced at the clock over the bar. "Time to go. Stay close to Steve. I can't worry about you and work."

"Fine." She kissed him again and left the booth after pretending to give him her phone number. She took a seat at the bar next to Steve and watched Drew saunter out the door.

"Where's Meaghan?"

"She said she had to work early tomorrow, so she left right after hooking you with your fiancé." Steve drained his wine. "I know you have a plan for keeping an eye on Drew."

"I do. We're drunk, we sneak out the back, and you have to pretend you can't keep your hands off me."

"You're killing me."

"Pretend I'm Meaghan and not your partner."

"I don't do drunk."

"Well, I'll do all the work then. You just have to stand there." She took his hand and pulled him down the hall toward the restrooms.

~

Oh, she wanted the cowboy very badly.

The man strolled from the bar with a long-legged stride

that made her legs weak and her palms sweat. Could she risk it?

No. The two detectives stumbled from the back of the bar and leaned against the wall. While they didn't appear to be watching the parking lot, Queen Coral knew they weren't really drunk. It was all a ploy to keep her from taking another man.

She slapped the steering wheel of her car. Perhaps, she could drive out of their sight and lean provocatively against her car. The cowboy might come to her instead of her going to him.

Turning the wheel, she drove to the far side of the lot where a street lamp flickered, ready to burn out. She exited the car, pulling her tight skirt to mid-thigh, then opened the hood. Cowboys were chivalrous. He'd come to her aid.

An older gentleman started toward her, and she shook her head and glared. He shrugged and continued to his vehicle.

The cowboy leaned against the building, one booted foot propped on the wall and peered from under his hat. Why wasn't he coming over? She bent at the waist, leaning further under the hood.

~

Drew chuckled as the redhead pretended to have car trouble. Something about her seemed familiar. If he went to help, he'd blow his cover. Unless…with a quick glance to where Linn hung all over Steve, something that would have driven Drew nuts a few months ago, he sauntered to the woman. "Howdy."

"Hello." She turned.

He blinked. "I saw you inside, with the wine drinker." He almost said her name. What was with the wig? "Need help?"

Her eyelids fluttered. She knew he recognized her. "Just a test. Obviously, one my boyfriend is failing."

Drew had no idea how to handle the situation. "Can I

give you a lift?"

"I think I have it." She slammed the hood down and pulled off the wig, allowing a cascade of dark hair to pour down her back. "I saw the way he looked at his partner this evening. Just wanted to know whether my premonitions were correct."

"They're cops?"

She nodded.

"Do you think they're doing a stakeout?" Drew put on a nervous face.

She shrugged.

"I'll catch you next time." He loped to his truck, hoping he looked guilty. If Linn tried to make him jealous the way this woman was doing Steve, there's be words between the two of them. He climbed into his truck, gave a small beep on the horn to alert his friend that he was being watched, then spun gravel from the parking lot. Another Friday night with nothing in his hand.

~

Steve glanced up, his heart threatening to pound through his chest from the way Linn was hanging on him. No matter how hard he tried, he couldn't shake his feelings for her. Meaghan?

She did not look happy. He peeled Linn's arms from around his neck. "Charade's over." He made quick time reaching Meaghan. "It's not what it looks like."

"You've been mooning over her all night when you thought I wasn't looking." She crossed her arms. "If you're working, why didn't you go after the cowboy? He looked very nervous at finding out you two were cops."

"We aren't looking for a man."

Her eyes narrowed. "That's why you only come here on Friday nights. Bars are not your thing, are they?"

"No. I prefer a restaurant and conversation I can actually hear. There are parts of my job you may not like, Meaghan. I really hope you'll see where this relationship takes us without cutting me off so soon."

"You aren't in love with your partner?"

"No." Yes. "We're just good friends."

She gave a slow, sexy smile. "Then, come home with me."

Linn was going to kill him. The rule was to never get involved with anyone during an investigation, but he couldn't resist the lure of the woman in front of him. He tossed his partner a wave and got into the passenger seat of Meaghan's car.

Thirty minutes later, they pulled up in front of an upscale apartment complex. Once inside, he glanced around, pleased at the stylish, white furniture with spots of red and black for color. "Nice place."

"Thank you. Make yourself comfortable. There's wine in the wine fridge in the kitchen. Pour us each a glass…your choice. I'm going to slip into something more comfortable." She shot him a coy look and disappeared down a hallway.

The kitchen was smal, but modern with stainless-steel appliances. Meaghan was right. It was time to let his partner go and focus on someone whose tastes were more like his own. He chose a bottle of red wine and found two glasses in a rack mounted under the cupboard.

He headed back to the living room and set the glasses on a coffee table, then sat on one end of the sofa, waiting for Meaghan. She didn't disappoint. She stepped into the room and he lost his breath.

Dressed in a sheer black negligee, the light from one lamp shining through and illuminating her curves, she smiled. "Satisfatory?"

"More than." Desperately needing something to replace the moisture in his mouth, he reached for his glass of wine. What was he doing? He didn't look at women casually. Obviously, Meaghan expected the night to end in the bedroom. Was he ready for that? If not, why had he come home with her? He had no car, little cash in his wallet—he was stuck.

"There is a range of emotions flickering across your face." She took the other wine glass. "Do you not want me?"

"I don't do…this. It has to mean something. I am attracted to you. Very much so. I think we might have something worth pursuing. I'm afraid of cheapening it before it's had a chance."

She sat next to him and placed a hand on his knee. "So, we talk."

She wasn't going to make it easy for him, was she?

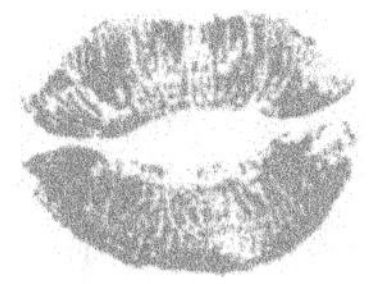

# Chapter Nine

"I cannot believe that with the deaths that are happening, Steve went home with a woman he'd had dinner with once. Once!" Linn held up a finger.

"Not the smartest thing, I agree." Drew handed her a cup of coffee, then sat behind his desk. "Last night was a total waste, but someone might as well get something out of it."

"Crude." She blew into her hot brew as the phone rang.

Drew grabbed the receiver. "Chief Wayne. Got it." He jumped up and grabbed his coat. "We've got a missing male from the next town. College age. His parents said he never came home two nights ago."

Normally, they'd assume he was hanging with friends, but with Queen Coral on the loose, they had to figure every disappearance was at her hands. Linn dumped her coffee and followed Drew. "Are you sure you want to go? Steve should be here any minute. We can handle it. I'm sure you have important paperwork to do." She grinned.

"Very funny. I miss this. Especially working with you." He snatched the keys from her hand. "I'm driving."

She grunted. Drew was the only one who could get away with that type of behavior. "It's a good thing you're cute."

The GPS navigator in Drew's truck took them to the residence of Bill and Susan Wells in forty-five minutes. The front door opened before they got out of the truck. A middle-aged couple with red-rimmed eyes stepped onto the porch.

"Are you here about Lance?" The woman asked, dabbing at her eyes with a tissue.

"Yes, ma'am." Linn flashed her badge. "May we step inside?"

The Wellses stepped back and let them enter, closing the door behind them. "Please, have a seat," Mr. Wells said. "Would you like water, tea, coffee?"

"Coffee, please." Linn smiled.

"Make that two." Drew placed a small handheld recorder on the coffeetable. "I'd like to record our conversation, if that's all right."

Mr. Wells nodded as his wife went to the kitchen. "Lance is a good kid. In college, a bit crazy about girls, gets good grades..." his voice choked. "He lives here to save expenses and always calls or texts if he's staying somewhere else for the night. I've tried calling, but now the phone is dead. No one ever answered."

"Where was your son on the night he disappeared?" Linn took the offered coffee. "Thank you."

"Out with friends for drinks is all he said."

"We'll need a list of his friends," Drew set his coffee next to the recorder.

"We called them. They said they didn't see anything."

"Sir, it's possible they saw something they don't understand the importance of."

"That Queen Coral has him, doesn't she? That's what the newspapers call her. A black widow who lures young men to their deaths." Mrs. Wells burst into sobs.

"Ma'am, we don't know that. Don't lose hope."

"Until there's a body, you mean," Mr. Nelson shook his head.

"We're doing everything we can to find your son."

Linn turned to the mother. "Can you make the list? A recent photo would also be helpful." Her phone buzzed. As Mrs. Wells fetched paper and a pen, she checked the text. From Steve wanting to know where she was and why she wasn't answering her phone.

She texted back that she was interviewing parents of a missing man and turned off her phone. They would catch him up when they returned. That's what he got for staying out all night as if he didn't have a job to do.

Mrs. Wells handed her a list of six names and a photograph she pulled from a drawer. It matched the one on the mantle. "Those are the only ones I know, and the picture was taken last month on his birthday."

"A girlfriend?"

"They broke up three months ago." She added the woman's name to the list. "Please, save my son."

"We'll do our best." Linn stood and shook their hands, while Drew turned off the recorder.

With more promises to help Lance Wells, they headed to the truck. "Do you want to check out the names now or have Steve and I do them?"

Drew turned the key in the ignition. "I want to check out the bars in the neighborhood. See if anyone recognized the victim. If…he is a victim."

The bartender at a seedy bar next to the freeway recognized him. "Yeah, him and a couple of other fellas were here. Had a lot to drink. This guy left first."

"Alone?" Linn took back the photograph.

"Yeah, but it seemed as if the other ones were looking for him. I think he went home with some gal."

"Why would you say that?"

"I was taking out the garbage when a blonde

approached him. He was drunk, but not so much he couldn't flirt. I didn't actually see them get into a vehicle because I came back inside. It was near closing time."

"What time was that?"

"Almost two."

"Thank you for your time." Linn followed Drew back to the truck. "Either it's the same woman who took Bill Nelson or we have two blondes taking off with men."

"It's possible Lance hooked up and isn't ready to leave."

"It's also possible he can't leave."

Drew sighed. "Let's proceed with that idea. We'll head back to the office and call the friends. See if we can't get them to come in to be interviewed. If we can't reach them, we'll track them down."

~

Steve sat, feet propped on his desk, and glared when the Linn and Drew entered the room. "Hopefully, you have something to add to the caseboard."

"Hello to you too." Linn pinned Lance's picture to the board. "This guy is missing. Taken by a blonde from a bar. Glad you could make it in today."

"Women take too long to get ready in the morning. I thought Meaghan had to be at work early, but her version of early is ten o'clock." That was the last time he'd let himself be without his own car.

Drew handed him two names. "Call these guys and see if they'll come in to be questioned. Linn and I will also call two, and Linn will call the ex-girlfriend. Maybe we'll get a lead."

Glad for something to do, Steve booted up his computer and started searching for phone numbers and addresses. "I have three Dave Morrows."

"He'd be around the age of twenty-one. A college buddy." Drew took the third desk, usually empty since the precinct ran on a skeleton crew. Which was why they hadn't caught the killer. "We need to call for help on this case."

"FBI coming in tomorrow," Drew said, not looking up from his computer. "Two agents will be assisting us. We'll give them our full support."

"Former friends of yours?" Steve wrote down a phone number.

"We're still friends."

The next hour was spent with the three of them asking potential witnesses to come into the office. Steve spent most of that with one finger in the ear not plastered to the receiver. Phone calls were hard enough with just Linn and him. Add in a third, and they were near impossible.

"I think we need to move the investigation into the conference room," Drew said. "I can't hear myself think."

A look of relief passed Linn's face. "I feel like a sardine." She stood and rolled the caseboard out of the room. The rattle of wheels on the tiled floor echoed.

Steve glanced at Drew. "Didn't take her long to move."

Drew laughed. "That's my girl. I wanted to thank you for not blowing my cover with your girlfriend."

"Is she a suspect?"

Drew's smile faded. "Everyone is a suspect." He left the room, leaving Steve to ponder his statement.

Meaghan wasn't a killer. Alluring, yes. Not overly fond of the male species, yes. But a killer? No. He'd stake his life on it.

In the conference room, they compared notes. Everyone had agreed to come in to be questioned except the missing man's ex-girlfriend. She, apparently, was on vacation. It was quite possible Lance had gone with her. Maybe they'd made up and disappeared to work on their issues. Still, Steve agreed with the others they needed to proceed as if Queen Coral had the man.

Their receptionist, Allie Maddock, a gal who didn't look old enough to be out of high school, entered the conference room. "Your first interview is here." She flicked her long blond hair out of her face. "He's quite a looker." She wiggled her eyebrows. "But rather obnoxious."

"How old are you?" Steve frowned.

"Twenty-five."

"Do you frequent bars?"

She looked taken back. "No more than the other gal. Why the interrogation?" Her eyes widened, then she burst into laughter. "You think I might be Queen Coral? That's a riot! I love men." Still laughing, she headed back to the front.

Steve shrugged. Didn't hurt to ask. "She does fit the profile."

"What profile?" Linn shook her head. "All we have to go on is a blond woman. Could be a wig. Could be strawberry, like my hair."

"It doesn't hurt to ask." Drew leaned back in his chair. "Who's going to interview our handsome guy?"

"Let Linn. We can watch through the two-way. If he's a flirt, a pretty woman will get more information out of him then we will," Steve said.

"Okay." Linn grabbed a tape recorder. "I should have worn makeup today if I'm going to use my beauty to get answers." She smiled, flipping her hair as Allie had done.

"Just stop." Steve returned her grin. "You know you're gorgeous with or without the face paint." He looked at Drew who studied him with an intense stare.

Once Linn left, Drew spoke. "You're still in love with her."

"No, I'm not." Steve fiddled with a pile of papers on the table.

"You are. I don't blame you, but I'm not looking forward to squaring off like we did six months ago."

"I told you, I've moved on." Steve met his stare. "Linn is yours. She'll always be yours. I do love her, but as a sister, a partner."

"Hmm." Drew stood. "Time to watch the show." He marched out of the room.

Did the chief really see Steve as competition? If Linn didn't love Steve with a romantic love by now, she never would. He was content with their relationship as it was.

~

"Hello, Darling." Queen Coral entered the basement.

"Please. No more," the man said, lifting his head. His dark hair fell forward over one eye.

"But, I'm frustrated." She pouted. "My next prey got away. I need to play."

She dropped her robe.

The man's eyes widened at her nudity.

"Don't worry. There won't be any blood or pain this time, maybe." She trailed one manicured finger down his sweating chest. "Isn't this why you came with me? Isn't this why all men chase after women? Are you disappointed your plan of a one night stand turned into something more?" She sighed. "Men. Disgusting creatures, really. Still, they can be fun. Do you think there are any that actually cherish women?"

"Which of those am I supposed to answer?" His gaze followed her until she stepped behind him. "Just let me go. I don't know who you are or what you look like."

"I'm not ready to let you go." She ran her fingers through his hair. "I rather like you. You're strong. Not one single whimper yet, except for your begging to let you go." She pinched his ear. "Which, by the way, is getting old. Don't let me tire of you. There are plenty more men out there."

"You're the woman who's been killing those men." His voice broke on the last word.

"Yes, that would be me." She returned to stand in front of him and leaned in closer, staring into his eyes. "See who you're dealing with? You might want to cooperate."

# Chapter Ten

Linn sat across from Dave Morrows--typical college kid—messy hair, messy clothes, killer smile. "I hope you don't mind if I record our conversation. Can I get you a bottle of water or coffee?"

"No, thanks." He glanced toward the mirror on the wall. "I'm not sure what I can tell you to help Lance, but I'll try."

"When was the last time you laid eyes on Lance?"

"At Freddy's Bar. We were celebrating his twenty-third birthday. He had a bit too much to drink and stepped outside for some fresh air." He leaned his elbows on the table. "The men's room was full, and I had to pis…you know, so I stepped out the back. I heard him talking to someone. At first, I thought he was talking to himself, but then I saw her."

Linn stiffened. "You actually laid eyes on the woman he left with?"

"I think so. I didn't see them get in the car."

"What did she look like?"

"Blond, almost white hair, tiny, curvy. Man, I could

only see the back of her, but I thought what a lucky gal Lance scored." He shook his head. "Not so lucky, huh?"

"Nope. Have you ever seen his ex?"

"Annie? Sure. It wasn't her. She's in Tijuana on vacation. Plus, she's part African American."

Linn groaned inwardly. They weren't learning anything new. "Can you remember any of the vehicles in the parking lot?"

"No, I was too drunk." He rubbed his hands over his face. "If I'd have known, I could have saved him."

"This isn't your fault." Linn pushed to her feet. "Please call if you think of anything else."

"Yes, ma'am." He gave a sad smile. "You're pretty for a cop."

She gave a curt nod. "You're okay for a college kid."

He laughed. "Touché detective." He left the room, calling out a greeting to someone.

Linn went to join Drew and Steve. "Nothing new."

"Confirmation that we're looking for a blond woman, possibly wearing a wig." Drew handed her a slip of paper. "Another friend is here. Chip Langley. He's heading in now."

"Coffee, please. I need it." She squared her shoulders and went back into the interrogation room. While she enjoyed questioning suspects and making them squirm, grieving family and friends turned the tables on her.

"Good afternoon, Mr. Langley. Coffee or water?" She sat down and pressed the on button to the recorder.

"Water, please."

Linn motioned to the mirror. Seconds later, Steve entered, handed the man the water, then left. This friend had seen less than the one before. When he finished talking, she thanked him and waited for the next one. By the end of the day, her head throbbed and her back hurt from the hard chair. Pounding the pavement was preferable to sitting all day.

She met up with Steve and Drew in the conference room where someone had ordered pizza. "Thank you!" She grabbed a large slice of sausage and cheese. "I'm starving."

"Hard work just sitting around, isn't it?" Drew planted a kiss on her cheek. "Let's eat, then make a game plan to present to the FBI in the morning." He pulled a laptop close to him. "I'm going to spend some time in the data base and see whether any blondes have a history of this type of behavior."

"I don't think the woman is blond," Linn said, wiping pizza grease from her hands, "but maybe one of the women you find will have committed crimes wearing a wig." It was a long shot, but stranger things have happened. "We need enough officers to hang out on a regular basis at every seedy bar and gentleman's club within an hour's drive."

"Wishful thinking."

"True, but it would help." She flashed him a grin.

"With The Photographer case," Steve said, reaching for his second slice, "the man was stalking Linn. Every day we got something from him to send us in a certain direction. This woman—she isn't playing by any rules but hers."

Linn almost wished for a car bombing. Anything to keep them active.

"Hello, Andrew Wayne." A very pretty brunette in a dark suit strolled into the room and landed a heavy kiss on Drew.

Linn's jaw dropped.

~

"Lauren." Drew stood. "You're early." He gave her a hug that lifted her off her feet. "Who's the brute standing behind you?"

"This is Bill Wilson, my new partner." When he released her she stepped back. "Handsome as ever, you are."

He held his hand out to Linn. "This is Linn, my fiancée, and her partner Steve Chavez. You'll be working closely with all three of us."

Lauren thrust out her hand. "Drew has told me a lot about you."

"He has?" Linn glanced at him.

"Sure, he has. During those long stakeout hours, that's all he talked about."

From the look on Linn's face, she was still skeptical. Six months apart, except for the occasional weekend, hadn't done much for their relationship. He intended to make up for the time away.

After filling the agents in on what little they had, Drew motioned for everyone to have a seat around the conference table. "We really have nothing but speculation. I did find a few recently released women known for killing men. All are blond except one, and she always wore wigs. Different colors and styles. Never the same one twice."

"Most abductees are dead within forty-eight hours," Lauren said.

"True." Linn folded her arms on the table. "But we've found the bodies of her other victims. The last man she kept for a while escaped. It's quite possible that Lance Wells is still alive."

Drew agreed, but it bothered him there'd been no more bodies. Had Queen Coral gone underground, satisfied with her latest prize? "We're treating the case as if he is. Agent Langley, we'll need you to go undercover this Friday at the club. Every other night of the week, you, I, and Steve will visit smaller bars. Eventually, we'll catch a break." He hoped. If God showed mercy, they'd catch this woman before too many more deaths piled up.

Allie stepped into the room. "That reporter, Alan, is here. He wants to speak with someone."

"I'll go." Drew stood. He wasn't ready for the public to know he'd brought in the FBI.

Alan stood in the waiting room, no camera, but held a clipboard, clearly ready to take notes. "Afternoon, Chief.

Mind if I ask you a few questions?"

"Ask ahead. We're planning a press conference in a day or two, so there are some things I'm unable to answer at this time." Drew had the reporter follow him to an empty office. "Have a seat, Alan."

The reporter sat. "Rather than me ask questions and get shot down, why don't you tell me what you're able to tell me."

"To the point. I like that." Drew grinned and crossed his arms. "We're dealing with a serial killer the papers have dubbed Queen Coral. She lures men from bars. Some she keeps, others she kills right away. I won't release the name of her latest victim until the press conference. We don't have a physical description of the woman other than that she is petite, curvy, and blond. Might be a wig. She takes her men around the time the bars close."

Alan's pen scratched across the surface of his notepad. "Anything else? I've gone to see Bill Nelson, but he refused to speak with me."

"Nothing I can do there." Drew leaned his elbows on the table. "Alan, don't investigate this. You're this woman's type."

"What is her type?"

"Young, handsome…"

"I'm an investigative reporter. It's what I'm paid for."

"Is it worth paying with your life?"

"I promise not to go home with any women I find at a bar." Alan stood. "Thank you, Chief. I can make a good article out of this. Please let me know when you have the press conference" He shook Drew's hand and left.

Drew really hoped it wasn't the last time he saw the eager reporter alive. He'd almost left out the part about Queen Coral taking her men from bars, but the public needed to be warned. He'd have done the same for women if the predator was male.

"Langley wants to requestion everyone you've already

questioned." Lauren leaned in the doorway. "He wants to see whether any stories have changed or new information remembered."

"It's a waste of time. No one knows anything. His time would be better spent talking to Bill Nelson if he wants to requestion." Drew didn't like his work second-guessed. Hopefully, he wouldn't have a problem with Agent Langley.

"Don't scowl." Lauren smiled. "Langley likes to be head rooster. He won't be on your turf long."

"He might. This case isn't going to be an easy one."

~

Queen Coral threw caution aside and pulled up to a bar she'd already visited once before. The moonless night cast everything in shadow. The streetlamps illuminated the seediness of the place.

She laughed, recognizing Upton Fall's reporter. Silly man. Didn't he know his face was recognizable? She dismissed him and turned her attention to the door, waiting for her possible prey.

Perhaps she should choose a man who was not Caucasian. Spice things up a bit. Rather than kill him right away, she could hold on to him. Have a variety in her underground lair. Yes! She loved that idea. Brilliant.

A tall, well-built black man exited the bar, stumbling a bit before righting himself. He'd be a challenge, but she welcomed the effort it would take to make him crack.

Opening her car door, she boldly approached the inebriated man. "Well, aren't you a fine-looking specimen."

He grinned, white teeth flashing against his ebony skin. "You looking for company?" His gaze raked over her.

"If you're up to it." She batted her eyelashes.

"I didn't see you inside."

"I saw you clear enough." She ran a fingernail down the buttons of his shirt. "Leave your car. I'll bring you back in the morning."

He glanced at a red Mustang convertible. "I guess. I'm in no shape to drive anyway." He pulled a car fob from his pocket and pressed it, making sure the vehicle was locked. "You live far?"

"Not too far." She smiled and walked away, swaying her hips. She glanced over her shoulder and noticed the bartender standing in the doorway. Her steps faltered, but she continued. He wouldn't be able to identify her. Not with the wig she wore and the distance between them.

Her prey followed her like a bear to honey. It was way too easy to make these men come with her. Just once, she'd like to use the syringe in her purse. Make them fight her, just a little.

Once they reached the warehouse, he balked. "Hey. Where did you bring me?" He turned and glared.

"Oh, darling, this is where the fun is." She stuck her hand in her purse and pulled out the syringe. "Follow me."

He eyed the needle and reached for the door handle.

She plunged the needle into his neck.

He went limp.

After unlocking the passenger door, she grabbed him under the armpits and dragged him inside the building. The man weighed a ton. She put on her mask.

"Sweetheart, I've brought you company," she sang, dragging her prize down the stairs. With great effort she tied him to a post, then stood back, panting. "I've decided to make a collection."

"You're sick." Lance glared. "How did you catch him? That man is a moose."

"A sway of the hips, a bat of the eyelashes. You're all the same." Disgusting. She was giving the world what it needed. Ridding it of filth one man at a time.

She perched on an empty crate and waited for her latest to awaken.

He groaned. His eyelids fluttered, then opened. He

struggled against his bindings.

It didn't take long for her to realize she needed to secure him better. "Settle down, big guy." She took a zip tie from a shelf and wrapped his hands behind the post. "Let's have some fun." She pulled her shirt over her head.

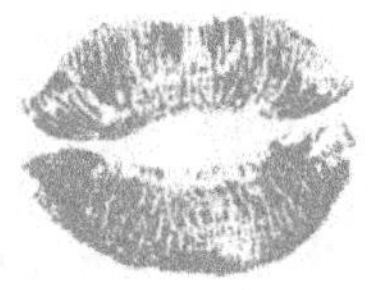

# Chapter Eleven

"Got another disappearance." Steve plopped a note on Linn's desk.

"Without us finding a body first?" What was happening? She typed the latest name into the computer and stared at the DMV photo of an attractive black man. "This isn't her MO."

Steve shrugged. "Want do you want me to say? His roommate said he didn't show up last night, and his car is still parked at the bar."

She prayed it was a simple *forgot the time with a pretty girl*. "Does Drew know?"

"He's waiting for us in the conference room."

After printing off Jamal Lincoln's picture, she took it and her coffee to the conference room. The mood was solemn. She tacked the picture on the caseboard and took her seat.

"We're starting our bar visits tonight. Linn, that means you, too. You and Lauren will go together and watch any man who leaves the bar alone." Drew speared her with a glance.

"We can cover more territory if we go alone. Queen Coral isn't looking for women."

"I don't want either of you alone. That's final. A caged animal attacks. Remember that."

She groaned and glanced at Agent Mayne, who shrugged. Linn hated undercover work at bars. Having once danced in one, she wanted to avoid that atmosphere at all costs. "We won't need to go to the one Jamal disappeared from other than to ask questions. It's doubtful she'll hit the same one two nights in a row."

"True," Drew said. "It's on the list for next week. Linn, you and I will question the bartender where Lincoln disappeared. Steve will go see the roommate. The agents will come with us and check out the abandoned vehicle. Let's go, folks. Queen Coral has stepped up her game. We need to do the same."

There wasn't much more to do than keep questioning people. Frustration boiled through Linn's veins. "I'll drive." She snatched the keys out of Drew's hand.

"I know you don't like having to go with Lauren," he said, buckling his seatbelt in the passenger seat of her jeep. "But, I can't worry about you."

"What about me worrying about you?"

"I'm on the offense."

"Did you see the size of Jamal Lincoln? She couldn't have subdued him without drugs. You can't stop a needle you don't see coming." She turned the key in the ignition and roared from the parking lot.

"We have to draw this woman into the open."

"I know that." She cut him a sideways glance. "I also know you're doing your job. That doesn't mean I have to like any of it."

"I felt the same way last year when Lyons was after you." He faced out the window.

Touché. "I'm sorry."

He grasped her hand. "Me, too."

Feeling better, Linn drove to a bar on the outskirts of town and showed the bartender her badge and a picture of the latest victim. "Recognize him?"

"Yeah, he's a regular. That's Jamal."

"Did he leave with anyone?"

The bartender, Ray, his nametag said, glanced from her to Drew, then back to her. "What's this about? Is he in some kind of trouble?"

"That's what we're here to determine." Linn kept her face impassive.

"No, he left with a woman. Jamal left his phone on the bar. I ran out to hand it to him when I saw him get into the car with some blonde."

"Did you get a good look at her?"

"Sure did. They were standing under a streetlamp. The woman looked right at me."

Linn exchanged a hopeful look with Drew. They may have gotten the break they needed. "Could you identify her from a photo?"

"Most likely. I'm good with faces. It comes in handy with my job."

Drew handed the man a folder with the mugshots of convicted murderers.

Ray paged through the photos. "None of these. This gal was a real looker. Stood about five foot two, worked out...definition in her arms...white hair. This is the part I'm not sure about. I think she had dark eyes but I can't verify that. Full lips, perfect nose. Heck, the woman could grace the cover of a magazine."

"Would you be willing to come to the station and speak with our forensic artist?" Drew asked.

Linn wasn't aware they had one. She fought to keep her surprise from showing on her face.

"Sure," Ray said. "I'll be there in half an hour. That's

when the next bartender comes in."

"Ask for an agent by the name of Mayne. She'll be glad to sit down with you." He put his hand on Linn's back and escorted her from the bar.

"Finally. We'll have a composite of our suspect."

"I didn't know Lauren was a composite artist."

"Used to be, before working for the FBI. She's the best we've got right now." He snatched the keys from her hand, throwing her a wink. "You're at a quarter of a tank."

"I planned on getting gas after work."

"We'll get it on our way to the station."

An ambulance raced past the bar, siren wailing.

Drew and Linn dashed for the jeep as the radio inside beeped. Linn grabbed the receiver. "McFarland here."

"Accident on Highway 64. Multiple vehicles," dispatch said. "Just past Hotchkins farm."

"On our way." She removed the flashing light from her glove compartment and set it on the roof of the jeep. "Let's go."

Paramedics were already there. Meaghan glanced up from where she helped hoist a man onto a gurney. Her eyes scanned the area.

"He hasn't arrived yet," Linn said, heading to where several people sat on the curb. Steve's woman friend had looked for him like a starving tiger drools over a pan of meat just out of its reach. She smiled, thinking of how she always looked for Drew. Her senses went on alert the moment he stepped in the vicinity. Her heart stuttered with one look from those eyes. Her skin rippled with every touch. Oh, yes, she knew the lure of a handsome man.

A Hispanic woman sat with her arms around two children under the age of twelve. She glanced up, her face clouded with worry. "Any news on my husband? His name is David Hernandez."

"I'll check on that for you." Linn squatted next to her. "What happened?"

"The motorhome over there started swerving, fell over, and slid, knocking into the other vehicles like dominoes. I'm a bit bruised, my kids shook up, but the driver's side door was crushed and Dave couldn't get out."

"The emergency team is working on getting him free." Linn glanced to where the fire department pried open the door to a minivan. The good-looking man inside turned his head toward his wife and gave a weak smile. "He looks like he'll be just fine." She stood and put a hand on the wife's shoulder. "I'll go check on him for you."

Linn approached the firemen and smiled at the man in the van. "You doing all right, sir?"

"My leg is pinned, but I'm good knowing my wife and kids are free." He grimaced as the firemen pulled the door open with a screech.

After a quick examination, they pulled him from the vehicle and lifted him to a stretcher. A gash the length of his thigh spurted blood. One of the paramedics put a tourniquet on him. "We'll have him sewn up in no time," the man said. "Tell the wife she can come along."

Linn nodded and went to relay the news. Before she'd completed her sentence, the family rushed to join Mr. Hernandez.

Smiling, she then went to join Drew where he helped the police from the next town over search the vehicles for bodies and survivors. Once they were satisfied the automobiles were empty, Drew led Linn to the side of the road.

"The old man driving the motorhome had a heart attack. Neither he or his wife made it." Drew shook his head. "Four fatalities and multiple wounded."

"Could have been worse." Linn headed for the jeep. "Let's see whether the bartender made it to the precinct." She really wanted a good look at the composite photo.

~

Queen Coral grinned and drove her latest prize to her

hidden place. What fun! She'd taken the handsome Hispanic right from under the noses of law enforcement. She was invincible. Oh, they'd find out her identity soon enough, but they'd never find her.

The drug she'd given her victim wore off as she struggled to get the man into a chair. Blood seeped through the bandage on his leg. First priority…stitch up his wound.

She smiled at the other two men. "Another for my collection."

The black man—she didn't like thinking her collection possessed names—said, "All you need now is an Asian and an Indian." He snarled, one finely chiseled lip curling.

"Oh, darling, it's all part of the plan." She knelt in front of her latest and reached for the first aid kit. Ignoring his groans, she expertly stitched the wound on his leg, then gave him a shot of antibiotics. "There you go. All better." She patted his face, then went up the stairs, locking the basement door behind her.

There wasn't a lot of time before the authorities would storm her residence in town. She needed to take a few things out before she left them a special gift.

At her apartment, she loaded a suitcase, grabbed her toiletries, and laid a negligee and the blond wig on the bed. She grabbed a remote from the dresser, set a timer, and hurried to a place thick with trees across the road where she could watch the show.

~

Steve paced the hall as the man named Ray described the woman with Jamal Lincoln to Agent Mayne. In a short while, they'd have a face to go with evil.

"How much longer?" Linn asked as she and Drew marched toward him.

"Almost finished." Steve glanced through the window of the conference room. "He keeps changing the shape of the mouth."

"We're finished," Agent Mayne called.

Steve hurried into the room and shook the witness's hand. "Thank you for your time." He lifted the picture from the table. No. It couldn't be. His heart stopped, his hand shook.

"What's wrong?" Linn peered into his face, then glanced at the picture. "That's the paramedic…your girlfriend."

"It has to be a mistake." Steve collapsed into a chair. "It's just someone who looks like her."

"No mistaking that face," Drew said.

Nausea rose in Steve's stomach. Why her? Why the first woman he'd expressed interest in other than Linn? "There has to be an explanation." He dug his cell phone out of his pocket and dialed Meaghan.

"Hello, darling."

How did he ask if she were a cold-blooded serial killer? No other way but outright. "Are you Queen Coral?" If he were wrong, he'd asked for forgiveness.

A few seconds of silence, then a strong answered, "yes, I knew you'd figure it out. You're a smart man. That's what I like about you."

"Why didn't you take me?" He closed his eyes.

"You're different than the others. You're a rare gentleman. Men are pigs, for the most part. It would be a shame to rid the world of one as fine as you."

"How many men have you taken, Meaghan?"

"How many do I have now or how many have I killed?"

Her question made his blood run cold. He barely heard Drew issue an APB.

"Both," he uttered, forcing the words past a throat swollen with despair.

"I've lost count of how many I've killed over the years, but I have three toys to play with. I'm looking for two more." She chuckled. "Ciao, sweetheart. It's been fun. I wish you wouldn't have figured out the puzzle so quickly." Click.

Linn grabbed the ringing phone, then looked up in alarm. "The ambulance David Hernandez was in is missing."

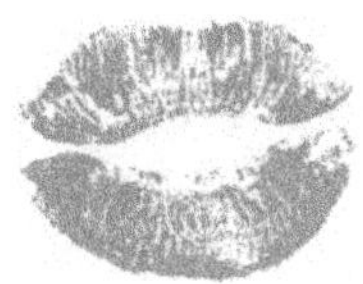

# Chapter Twelve

"I'm sorry, Steve." Linn dropped her purse on her desk and hung her suit jacket over the back of her chair. "No one suspected Meaghan." The dejected look on his face ripped at her heart.

"Some detective I am." He shook his head. "I've got a serial killer right next to me and I can't see past her pretty face."

"Just be glad you aren't one of her victims." Linn sat in her chair. Meaghan had said she was collecting rather than killing right now. Maybe they had time to save the three men she held. What did she do with the ones she held on to? Tortured, they knew, but why did she keep some longer than others? Her kidnapping was escalating.

"Where's Drew?" Steve's question drew her attention back to him.

"Brainstorming with the FBI." As the new chief of Upton Falls, better him than her. Linn rarely did forensic work anymore, focusing her time on chasing the bad guys, or girls, in this case. "Let's go talk to the family of David Hernandez."

"They won't know anything."

"Probably not, but it beats sitting here." She stood and grabbed her jacket and purse. "Are you coming?"

He sighed and got to his feet. "Let's go."

He wasn't going to argue with her about who was driving. Poor Steve. He had it bad for that woman.

"Forget whatever it is you're doing." Drew rushed into the room. "Kevlar vests on. We have an address."

Linn glanced at Steve. Normally, when they were this close to bringing down the perp, they exchanged huge grins. Not today. Instead of anticipation, pain flickered across his light green eyes.

Last year the twin brother he hadn't known he'd had wanted Linn. Was obsessed with her. Was the man who had raped her years ago. Now, Steve finds a woman he actually likes and she's also a killer. Linn pressed her lips together and pulled a vest from a hook on the wall. She tossed one to Steve, then donned her own.

"SWAT will go in first," Drew explained as they rushed to the van. "We'll hold back and take care of the victims."

"I get Meaghan." Steve marched ahead of them.

"You can have her," Linn said. Her partner deserved to be the one to slap the cuffs on the woman.

Outside, they climbed into the back of the department van and followed the SWAT team to a modest neighborhood on the other side of town. While they drove, they put on earpieces.

Putting an end to a dangerous killer filled her with adrenaline. Things could go smooth or very messy. Linn was praying for easy, but her gut told her Queen Coral wouldn't go down without a fight.

The van stopped at the end of the street while police put up barricades to lessen the amount of neighbors wanting to get close. It didn't take long for the news to arrive. Alan Barker, followed by his camera crew, tried to cross the barrier.

"Come on. You can't keep out the media."

"We can and we will," Linn told him. "It's for your safety. The chief will give a statement at the first opportunity. Until then, do nothing more than take your pictures." She gave him a look that should alert him to the fact she wouldn't accept an argument. When he started to open his mouth, she held up a finger.

"You're cold, Linn."

"I've been told that before." She joined Drew and Steve in front of the van.

"It's too quiet." Drew crossed his arms and stared at the brick house. "It's obvious we're here and I haven't seen so much as a twitch of the curtains."

"What's the next move?" Linn asked. An icy fist gripped her heart.

"SWAT's going in." Drew moved toward the house.

"Stop. Something doesn't feel right." Linn had learned to trust her gut, and this was too easy.

The first SWAT member stepped onto the porch.

The house exploded.

Things seemed to happen in slow motion as Linn's mind registered the facts.

Drew was blown into the side of the van.

The explosion slammed Linn and Steve against the vehicle.

She slid to the asphalt.

Someone screamed.

Fire licked at the sky.

Linn got to her hands and knees and crawled to Drew. He didn't respond to her touch, nor was he breathing. "Drew!" She patted his cheek. No response. She straddled his middle and began chest compressions. "Come on, baby. Don't do this." Tears poured down her cheeks.

~

"We need an ambulance!" Steve pushed to his feet and took control. SWAT members were scattered across the front lawn like a child's forgotten toys. He tried to keep an eye on Linn in case she needed him, but with Agent Wilson down and Agent Mayne wounded, there was little of him to spare.

Some of the onlookers held hands to bleeding wounds. The explosion had blown glass and debris into the crowd and shattered windows of neighboring houses. Hell, they needed a fleet of ambulances. "Barker, shut off that camera and make yourself useful. People need help."

The reporter nodded, tightening his tie around his arm. He motioned for the cameraman to set down the equipment. Soon, they were wandering through the crowd separating the more gravely wounded from those who didn't need immediate attention.

Steve walked among those on the lawn, looking, hoping, but not finding, survivors. Ten of Little Rock's finest dead. What about Meaghan's victims? Were they burning to death under the rubble? Out of reach of help until it was too late?

He stopped in front of what used to be a house. Now nothing more than a scarred foundation. Since he didn't see any signs of a basement, he held onto hope that she kept her prisoners somewhere else.

"Steve!"

He whirled and raced to Linn's side.

"He's breathing. Help me get him to a sitting position."

Steve propped his shoulder under Drew and shifted the big man until he sat against the van. "You all right?"

Drew blinked, then nodded. "Thanks to my girl. I'm fine. Go help the others."

"Are you sure?" Linn cupped his face.

"I'm sure."

She nodded and stood. "What do you want me to do, Steve?"

"There isn't much to do. Most law enforcement personnel are dead. You can help keep control of the crowd."

She rushed to do his bidding, barking orders to those who were uninjured. When the ambulances arrived, she approached them.

Steve glanced one more time at the house, then Drew, then went to help the wounded.

~

"You are a darling." Meaghan watched the monitor. Putting a camera on the roof across the street had been one of her brightest ideas. She was able to watch the fun and Steve. Oh, he thought she was letting him off the hook, but no. He would be her final acquisition. She'd looked for a man as kind and gentle as him her entire life. Now that she'd found him, she did not intend to let him go.

She also wanted the hunk sitting against the van, but with no way to snatch him without being seen, she'd have to let him go. For now. Wouldn't his woman hate her if she took her man?

Meaghan laughed. She hadn't had this much fun in her entire life. Look at all the men she'd rid the world of. Women should thank her. She was doing them a service.

Watching the explosion and resulting carnage stirred up an itch. She clicked off the camera and went to have some fun with her toys.

~

"I said take me last." Drew pushed the paramedic's hand away. "I'm fine. There are others who need you more."

"Sir, you were dead. Detective McFarland resuscitated you. That requires medical attention."

"I'll go last." He scowled. What did the man not understand? "I'm sitting here like a worthless lump. The same thing I'd be doing at the hospital. That reporter has a piece of glass sticking out of his arm and from the pallor on his face, has lost a fair amount of blood. Take him. Or that woman in the housedress that keeps clutching her arm. You can't see blood, but I bet her heart is bothering her. Send my fiancée over her and get out of my face."

Shaking his head, the paramedic left. Less than five minutes later, Linn sat next to Drew. "Why are you being so obstinate?"

"How are you? Did you get hurt?"

"I'll have some bruises, and I've got a killer headache, but Steve and I weren't thrown as far as you. There's nothing left of the house."

"Victims?"

"Doesn't look as if she kept them here. Of course, once forensics scours the neighborhood for body parts we'll have a better idea, but I don't think they were here."

Drew glanced at the house. He wanted to go investigate, but any sudden movement made him want to vomit. It was best he stay put and pretend he didn't need the hospital as badly as everyone said he did.

He tried to pull his attention back to what Linn was saying. Her face swam in front of his eyes.

"Drew?"

He slumped over as darkness overtook him.

He woke in a hospital room, Linn sitting in a chair next to him. "Hello, handsome."

"Whoa, I'm nauseous." He grabbed the plastic bowl on the rolling table next to him. "How long have I been here?"

"Only a few hours. They treated me and Steve for concussions. Well, you too." She grinned. "You've got all the nurses in a frenzy rushing around trying to save the brave, handsome, chief of police. I'd be jealous if my head didn't hurt so bad."

Trying not to move his head, he shifted his gaze to rest on her face. "Is everything else all right? No permanent injuries?"

"Nope. Except the nurses won't let me stay with you. Something about hospital rules. Stupid people." She leaned forward and kissed him. "You sleep well and behave. Stop giving everyone a hard time. They only want to make you better. I'll see you tomorrow. I love you."

"Then kiss me again."

She laughed and pressed her lips to his. "Yes, I do believe you're going to be okay." She caressed his face, her hands warm. "Until morning."

"I'll be here." In fact, he couldn't wait to close his eyes again."I love you, darling."

"Ditto." She smiled and moved stiffly from the room, obviously in more pain than she'd let him believe.

They'd all be sore for a few days. It wasn't the first time Drew was laid up in the hospital. But, it was the first time he'd actually had his heart stop. That was a sobering thought. Steve may want to be the one to arrest Queen Coral, but Drew wanted a chance at her, too. Not only had she almost killed him, but she could have permanently taken Linn away from him.

After The Photographer last year, losing Linn had become Drew's greatest fear.

# Chapter Thirteen

Meaghan pushed a bed down the hall and passed the handsome chief of police's room. She hadn't planned on taking him, she really hadn't, but the man was too beautiful no to add to her collection. Once she had him, Steve, and the last two ethnic groups, she could stay home and play all day. It almost took more willpower than she possessed to keep a grin from spreading across her face.

The curly black wig, green contacts, and fat suit made her unrecognizable to anyone looking for her. In fact, she was able to ditch the bed and wheel an old woman down the hall to the nurse's desk. Even those stupid women didn't question her. Meaghan might have been missing a potential hunting ground by not frequenting hospitals.

She strolled the halls, casually glancing at name plaques near the doors. Kevin Cho. Ah. She peeked inside. A toothless old man gave her a wave. She scowled and moved on, not being able to resist laying eyes on the chief.

He stared up at her through drug-hazed eyes. A five o'clock shadow graced his strong jaw. The man was too handsome to belong to anyone but her. She smiled and fluffed his pillows, pulling the blanket up around his waist. "I've got other patients, handsome. I'll see you later."

Another name plaque down the hall stopped her. Bill Begay. She stepped into the room on the pretense of filling the water pitcher and grinned. A handsome Navajo man in his mid-twenties blinked up at her. The poor thing was obviously very medicated. This was going to be too easy.

"Let me help you into a wheelchair." She pulled down the blankets and grimaced. No man with a leg that ended at the knee was good enough for her. "Nevermind. Mistaken identity." Any marks or injuries on a man had to come from her.

A man strolled down the hallway as if he didn't have a care in the world. Bill Nelson, the only one who'd ever gotten away from her. She snuck up behind him on soft nurse shoes and pulled a syringe from the shirt pocket of her scrubs. "Mr. Nelson, are you being released today?"

"Yeah? Hey." He turned to run.

She inserted the needle into his neck, then caught him as he slumped over. With little effort, she got him into a wheelchair, waving away an orderly who had run over to help. "He's fine. Just a little dizzy. I've got him."

She glanced back toward Chief Wayne's room. Later, sweetheart. I've something to stash away first.

Ten minutes later, an unconscious Bill was tied up in the back of her van. She smoothed her rumpled scrubs and risked another trip into the hospital. She'd injected her latest with enough medicine to keep him out for an hour.

A cop sat outside Chief Wayne's room. Meaghan cursed. She might not be able to get him that day, but his day would come.

Giving up for now, she hurried back to the van and drove her prize home.

~

Linn settled into her desk chair and sipped her coffee. Her entire body ached. All she wanted to do was take Drew home and curl up on the sofa. But, with a serial killer on the loose, that day would have to be pushed sometime into the future.

Her desk phone rang. A glance at the clock told her the receptionist had left for the day, and calls were being forwarded. She sighed and answered.

"Detective McFarland."

"This is Doctor Mobley. I have a very frantic family here who says their son was abducted…again. A Bill Nelson. They insisted I call you. I'm pulling up security video as we speak."

"Hold on to it until I get there." She hung up, grabbed her coat and holster, and dashed out the door, almost knocking Steve over in the process. "Queen Coral struck again. Come on."

He tossed his Styrofoam cup of coffee into the nearest garbage can and raced after Linn. She tossed him the keys to her car. "I'm too sore to drive."

He raised his eyebrows. "If you're voluntarily letting me drive, you must feel pretty bad."

"Shut up and get in the car." Linn yanked open the door, got in, and had her seatbelt fastened before Steve had the key in the ignition.

Meaghan had been at the hospital. She'd guarantee it. That had put Drew in grave danger. There was absolutely no way Linn would believe Nelson was taken by anyone other than Queen Coral. She also doubted he'd left on his own without telling his family.

While they drove, she phoned Drew's room. "Are you all right?"

"Yeah." He sounded groggy. "What's wrong?"

"We believe Meaghan was at the hospital. Bill Nelson is missing."

"Wait. Slow down. Repeat that. I'm a little out of it because of the pain meds."

"Have you seen anyone other than me and your

doctor?"

"A chubby nurse, my regular nurse…that's it."

Steve parked close to the hospital entrance.

"We're going to look at video footage. I'll come by your room when we're finished. I love you."

"Love you, too. Be careful."

Linn hung up and exited the car, almost jogging to the hospital's entrance. She didn't have to wait for Steve. She knew from experience that her partner would be right behind her.

"We're here to see a Doctor Mobley." Linn approached the front desk.

A man came from a side room. "I'm he. Come on in. I've pulled up the footage from today, but haven't looked at it as you've requested."

"Thank you." Linn sat in a chair in front of the monitor. "May we have some privacy?"

"Sure." He frowned but left the room, closing the door behind him.

Steve leaned over Linn's shoulder as she scanned through the video. "There." He pointed. "Bill just signed something at the counter. I think he was being released."

Linn punched some keys and brought up the hall by Drew's room. Several nurses went in and out of his room, including an overweight woman. No one looked the least bit suspicious. She scanned through another video and found Nelson again.

"Look." She glanced up at Steve. "It's that nurse. She's---" As she watched, the nurse plunged a hypodermic needle into Nelson's neck, then supported his weight as she took him from the hospital. Right before they exited, she looked at the camera and smiled. "That's definitely Meaghan. She was in Drew's room." An icy fist squeezed her heart.

"Something must have kept her from taking him," he said.

"We need a guard posted. We can't take the chance on her returning." She pushed back her chair and headed for the door. "Grab the video, please. I'm going to see Drew."

"I'll catch up." He sat in the chair she'd vacated.

She nodded and left, hurrying to Drew's room. He sat propped up in bed, idly surfing channels on a muted television. When she sat next to him, he turned off the TV.

~

"Talk to me." Drew couldn't miss the fear reflecting in Linn's eyes.

She explained how his nurse had really been Meaghan. How she'd taken Bill Nelson again. How she'd smiled at the camera. All after having been in Drew's room.

"How did she act when she came in?" Linn's gaze locked on his.

He blinked, trying to clear his head. "Friendly. I thought there was something familiar about her, but the hair and green eyes threw me off. She smiled and said she'd see me later." He hated lying here like a helpless baby. No more pain meds. He'd fight through the pain. "I have to get out of here."

"We're going to post a guard outside your room."

"I'm the only one who can authorize that, and I won't." He tossed back the blankets, wincing against the pain in his head. "I'm getting out of here. We need to catch her before she kills Bill Nelson."

He clutched the back of his gown closed, grabbed his things from the small closet, and shuffled into the bathroom. "Go find the doctor," he yelled.

"Fine, but I think you're acting in haste."

Regardless, Drew would be better help in the investigation if he were out of the hospital and back at work. The headaches would subside, so would the body aches. Lives were more important than a few bruises.

When he'd finished, he met his doctor and a sullen Linn at the nurse's desk. "This is against my better judgment," the doctor said. "But this little lady tells me there's no talking you out of leaving."

"No, sir. I'm out with or without your permission." Drew spotted Steve exiting a small room. "Am I right?"

"I'm staying out of this one." Steve gave a wry smile. "I studied the videos more in depth and didn't find out anything more. Nelson recognized Meaghan right before she injected him, but that's all I got."

Drew scribbled his name on the release papers. "What about outside surveillance?"

Linn glanced at the doctor. "I didn't see any."

The doctor muttered something under his breath. "Excuse me. Wait right here." He marched to another room and immediately slammed the door. From his raised voice he was subjecting someone to a stern lecture. A few minutes later, he handed a jump drive to Drew. "Idiot left it on his desk. My apologies."

"Not necessary," Linn said. "I should have thought to ask."

"I'm surprised neither you or Steve thought of it." Drew frowned, his head already beginning to pound. "I know you're worried about me, but stop. I'm another officer right now. Not your fiancé." He entered the room Steve had exited and inserted the drive into a computer.

Linn and Steve stood behind him as he fast-forwarded through the video. "There." Linn tapped the screen.

A clear picture of Meaghan putting a drowsy Bill Nelson into the back of the van filled the screen. She closed the door, tossed her wig into a garbage can, and sped away from the hospital. Drew peered closer but couldn't make out the license plate. "Have the lab blow this up. It might give us something to go on. God knows we have very little."

He handed the jumpdrive to Steve. "Meet you at the station."

"We rode together." Linn put a hand on his arm. "Your

car isn't here."

"Right." He needed to keep his mind focused or Linn would smother him the same way he would her if the roles were reversed. "Let's go. We need to have a meeting with Mayne and Wilson."

"No one told you?" Steve shook his head. "Wilson was killed when the house blew. They haven't replaced him yet. I haven't spoken with Mayne. I'm not even sure she's still here."

"What do you remember, Drew?" Linn peered into his face.

"Not a lot, apparently." He exhaled sharply. "You can fill me in on the way."

Steve drove them to the station where Drew headed straight for the conference room. A sad-looking Agent Mayne sat alone at the table. "You did stay," he said.

"I have a job to do. They're sending me a new…partner." She studied his face. "Should you be here? I mean, you died."

"That's what I say." Linn plopped into a chair. "But he won't listen to me."

Drew took his seat and filled the agent in on what had transpired at the hospital. "Since Nelson had escaped her once, I don't hold out a lot of hope for his survival. I think she'll kill him out of spite and to keep the other men in control."

"I agree," Linn said, twirling a pencil between her fingers. "If she hasn't already killed him. We don't know what was in that syringe."

Steve shook his head. "No, if that was the case, she would have left him to die in the hospital. She has a plan before she kills him. We need to find out what it is before it's too late."

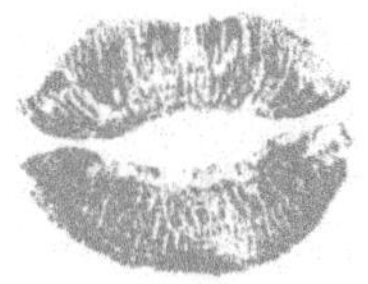

# Chapter Fourteen

"Dear, dear Bill." Meaghan tapped his cheek too hard to be anything but a warning. "You were a very bad boy. Do you know what happens to bad boys?"

Wide eyes stared over a gag in the man's mouth. He shook his head and mumbled something indecipherable.

"What?" She bent over him. "Are you begging? That isn't very manly of you." She should have let him go or killed him at the hospital. What did she need him for? She was going to have the chief of police and sweet Steve. "I ought to kill you know. All of you." She waved her arm and paced the damp basement smelling of sweat and fear.

She was tired of feeding, bathing, and providing a bucket for them to relieve themselves. It was hard, disgusting work. She stopped and stared at her collection. Such beautiful men. Four. Three more would make the perfect number. She twisted her lips. "I really want an Asian and a Native American. And the chief and Steve." She tapped a long scultured nail against her lips "That means two of you have to go." She sighed.,

The men stared at her as if they were statues, their eyes

watching her every move. Oh, the power! Two Causian. One young and delightfully accommodating. Precious Lance. Oh well, Bill had to go.

She grabbed a knife from a nearby table and sliced his throat before the man had time to scream behind his gag. She wiped the blade on his shirt. "That's what happens to bad boys. I'll take care of the body in a bit." She moved to Lance and ran her fingers through his hair. "Would you be a good boy and escort me to my room?"

He nodded, his eyes shimmering with unshed tears.

"Wonderful." She cut the zip ties around his ankles, then slipped her arm through his. "I won't free your hands, darling, but you won't need them anyway." She smiled at the others over her shoulders, faltering a second at the chilling look in Jamal's face. She hoped the big man wouldn't be a problem. He was one of her favorites. She laughed. They were all her favorites.

~

Linn studied the list of names in front of her. Lance Wells, twenty-one, Bill Nelson, thirty-five, Jamal Lincoln, twenty-seven, and David Hernandez, thirty-eight. A range of ethnic groups and ages. She really didn't think Meaghan was going to stop anytime soon, not after her unsuccessful attempt at abducting Drew. She was also certain the woman would try again.

She glanced to where Drew stood in the hallway talking to Agent Mayne. The crease between his eyes told her he had a headache. He'd made it clear she wasn't to baby him. So, how was she supposed to keep him safe?

"Frowning causes wrinkles." Steve leaned over her shoulder, a sad smile on his face.

"I don't know where to go from here." She tapped the list of names. "Do we start over by interviewing family and friends again? They're going to start slamming doors in our faces. Another trip to the bars would be a waste of time. How do we find Meaghan?"

"I've been working on that. Do you want to come with me to question her co-workers?"

"Sure. Give me a minute." She pushed away from her desk and approached Drew and the agent. "Steve and I are going to the fire department. Are you leaving the precinct?"

He chuckled. "No, sweetheart. I'll be safe and sound here with Agent Mayne trying to dig up a clue. Maybe you and Steve will have some luck."

"Hopefully." Her gaze fell to his lips. It would be unprofessional to kiss him in front of the agent. "May I speak with you in private for a moment?"

His smile widened, as if he could read her mind. "Excuse us, Agent." He led Linn into his office and closed the door, then pulled the blinds. "We've never fooled around at work before."

"We've never had you die before." She wrapped her arms around his neck. "I've never been this scared before."

"I won't leave you." His arms snaked around her waist and he pulled her close, lowering his head.

For a few minutes, she forgot the outside world as his lips caressed and teased hers. A knock at the door brought them to reality.

"We'll pick back up when we get home." Drew planted one more kiss on her lips, then opened the door.

Steve heaved a sigh. "Seriously? We have men dead and several still missing, and you two are making out like teenagers."

"How do you know?" Linn tapped his shoulder. "Peeking?"

"What else could it be?" He dangled her keys. "Who's driving?"

"Me." She snatched them from his hand, blew Drew a kiss, and marched to her car.

~

"It's not always a good thing to have a relationship with someone you work with." Agent Mayne raised her eyebrows. "When they're gone, you still have to work."

"I'm sorry about Agent Wilson."

"We were friends, but two years ago, I did work with my husband. He died in a raid on a house where two women were being held in a shed in the back yard. No one survived."

Drew opened the door to the conference room, surprised to see someone seated at the table. "Who are you?"

"Agent Chang." He held out his hand. "It's a pleasure to meet you." He turned to Agent Mayne. "You must be my partner."

She nodded. "I'm not sure you're the best one for this job."

He blinked several times. "Why not?" He resumed his seat and crossed his arms. "I heard you were easy to work with."

"It isn't that." She sat across from him, leaving the seat at the end for Drew. Leaning her elbows on the table, she fixed her gaze on Chang, then on Drew. "Hear me out."

Drew nodded, interested in what she could say that would appease her new partner.

"Queen Coral has two white men, one black man, one Hispanic. What is she lacking in her collection? I believe she wants a diverse ethnic group. That means she—who is she missing? Unless she has someone we don't know about she needs—"

"An Asian and a Native American." Drew scribbled the list on a piece of paper. "It also means that either Bill Nelson or Lance Wells are not needed. But, if she had her Caucasian, why try to take me from the hospital."

Chang cleared his throat. "Don't take this in the wrong way, sir, but you are a very attractive man. Not only that, but you are leading this investigation. You would make a treasured piece in her collection." He transferred his attention ot Mayne. "If the Queen is looking for an Asian man, I say we make it easy for her."

"Absolutely not." Drew shook his head. "We have no idea what she does to her victims. I'm sure it isn't pleasant."

"I'm a trained agent. I can handle a woman who collects men like a child collects toys."

"You can't stop a bullet, a bomb, or a knife to the throat if your hands are tied." Drew stood and pointed at the caseboard. "That's what she does to her victims when she tires of them."

"I've studied the board and read the reports."

"Then you know the idea is ridiculous," Mayne said. "You'd be better used tracking the woman down."

"Wait a minute." Drew leaned against the table, his gaze on the caseboard. "She hasn't killed one of the men in awhile. Maybe it isn't her intent to kill them as long as they cooperate. If Chang were to be captured, he could comply and look for a way to take down Meaghan."

"Or he could die like Wilson."

"That was an unfortunate accident. Our killer wasn't targeting any specific person." Drew cocked his head. "She also seems to want me. If Chang and I were both taken—"

"I need a cup of coffee." Mayne yanked open the conference room door. "Allie, coffee, please!" She turned back to Drew. "Neither one of you are acting on this harebrained idea without permission from the director. And you, Chief, should consult Detective McFarland."

Drew scowled. "I will certainly discuss this with her, but she understands we have a job to do." Linn would see the wisdom in setting a trap.

"You don't understand a woman in love at all, sir. No disrespect." She accepted the cup of hot coffee from Allie. "Thank you. I think these two need one as well."

Allie nodded. "There is a vehicle out front that won't stop honking."

Drew glanced at Chang, grabbed his holster, and rushed

from the room, followed closely by the two agents. "Everyone stay away from the doors," he yelled as he raced through the reception area.

He stopped at the front glass doors and eyed a black SUV idling in the parking lot. The horn let out one continuous blast.

"A trap?" Chang asked.

"Something to lure out thick-headed lawmen?" Mayne asked, smirking.

"Not sure." Drew glanced at Allie. "Call the bomb squad."

"That will take an hour. You know they have to come from Little Rock."

"I'm well aware of that." Why was everyone questioning his decisions? He rubbed his temples.

"Perhaps you should sit down." Mayne's fingers curled around his arm.

"I'm fine. This has nothing to do with my hospital stay." He glared at everyone within sight. "Got it? I. Am. Fine. Stop treating me like an invalid." He stared back at the SUV.

It looked as if someone were slumped over the steering wheel, which would cause the continuous honk. "I'm going out."

He opened the front doors of the precinct and stepped into the afternoon sunshine. He glanced heavenward and prayed for protection. If he got blown to bits, Linn would kill him. Taking a deep breath, he marched toward the automobile.

Chang cursed behind him. "This is the second dumb idea of the day."

"The first one was yours." Drew stopped a few feet away. There was definitely a body inside.

He squatted and peered under the vehicle. "Nothing that looks like a bomb."

"Maybe it's inside," Mayne said.

"I'm not going to open the door," Chang stated.

Drew squared his shoulders and reached for the handle. He slowly opened the door. When an explosion wasn't the result, he felt for a pulse on the man inside. Nothing. He leaned the man back against the seat, effectively stopping the horn.

"Bill Nelson." He glanced at the agents.

"I guess she narrowed her Caucasians by one." Chang moved closer. "Because he escaped?"

"That's my guess." Drew pulled the radio from his belt and told Allie to also call for the ME. This could very well be the result if he and Chang used themselves as bait.

Of course, there was always the chance Meaghan wouldn't kill them. She most likely killed Nelson because of his escape, as Chang had stated. The men who behaved…lived. Could Drew follow the instructions of a mad woman? Could he be unfaithful to Linn in order to stay alive? No.

He had a tough decision to make. Stay secluded and out of Meaghan's grasp or put himself, along with Chang, into her lair.

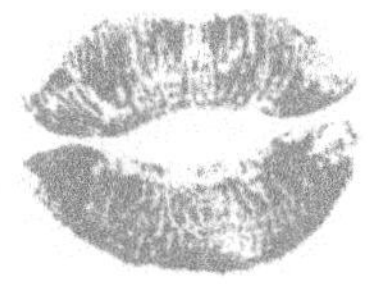

# Chapter Fifteen

Linn sat in the fire station across the table from the three EMTs Meaghan had worked with. In the center of the table rested a small tape recorder. "I hope you don't mind if we record our questions."

"Not at all." Mark Bailey, the one who appeared to be in charge, said. "We're shocked that Meaghan is the one killing these men."

"She seemed so sweet." Sharon Morrall, the only woman of the three, wiped her eyes with a tissue.

Linn cut a sideways glance at Steve. Was Morrall going to cry through the interview or be useful? Time was of the utmost importance. They couldn't waste it consoling a co-worker.

"None of you were at all suspicious of Miss Larson's behavior?" Steve opened a notebook.

Bailey shook his head. "She was a model employee, always putting the patient's needs first. Very nurturing."

"She did like the good-looking men, though." Larry Box, the third EMT spoke up. "I've seen her at a bar now and then. Men flocked around her like hummingbirds to nectar. She relished the attention."

"Did you ever see her in disguise?" Linn speared the man with a glance.

"Once." He tore a napkin into tiny pieces, making a paper mountain in from of him. "It's hard to miss a woman like her."

"Didn't it occur to you to say something when the news asked for information of a female predator?" Why were some people so dense?

"I didn't believe for a second that Meaghan could be the woman the authorities were looking for." He scooped the pile of napkin pieces into his hand and got up to throw them away.

Linn folded her arms on the table. "Anything else?" She looked from one to the other as Box resumed his seat. "Family property? Friends you've heard mentioned?"

The three sat quiet, seemingly deep in thought. None of them looked as if they were hiding anything. She'd worked here for five years. Someone had to know something to give them a lead as to what their next step could be. A woman like Meaghan Larson would never be invisible. Someone out there had seen her. Knew where she is.

"She did mention her family owning some land in the mountains," Morrall said, "but she never said exactly where, so I didn't think much of it."

The Ozarks covered hundreds of acres. Anyone with any experience in the wild could virtually disappear if they wanted. Linn waited for someone to had to what Morrall had said. When they didn't, Linn stood. "Thank you for your time. Please call if you remember anything at all." She handed each of them a business card.

When they had returned to her car, she turned to Steve. "Do you think this is enough information to warrant Drew having a copter fly around the mountains?"

Steve shrugged. "We found The Photographer without doing so."

"Because the woman who escaped knew where he kept the others." She started the car and headed for the precinct. A few miles down the road, her cell phone rang. She pressed the button to answer over Bluetooth. "Detective McFarland."

"This is Larry Box. I have information. Meet me at the corner of 23rd and Preston." Click.

Linn did a quick U-Turn. "Finally. Something that might help us get a step ahead."

"Be careful. It could be a trap."

She gave him a quick glance. "For what purpose? Larry Box doesn't fit the profile of the type of men Meaghan takes. He has no reason to help her."

"Let's just be on our guard."

When they reached their designation, Larry Box pointed to a nearby coffee shop. By the time they'd parked, he was sitting at a bistro-style table under the shade of a magnolia tree.

"Thank you for coming." He glanced around. "I couldn't speak in front of the others. I'm not the complete idiot you must think I am after finding out I didn't say anything about seeing Meaghan at the bar." He reached into his pocket and pulled out a tube of lipstick. "This was found when I cleaned out Meaghan's locker."

"So?" Linn leaned back in chair. "We already know she wears that shade."

He gave a sly smile. "And this was found after Sharon Morrall spilled her purse." He set a matching tube on the table.

"They can't be the only two women in Upton Falls to wear that shade." Linn chewed the inside corner of her mouth. Using a napkin, she picked up one of the tubes and read the manufacturer's name before handing it to Steve. "This manufacturer only makes custom colors. A client blends the lipstick she likes and they make it for her. Very expensive."

He shrugged. "And?"

"Only one person has each shade. There are no duplicates. The only way Sharon could have gotten this exact color was if Meaghan gave it to her."

The proverbial lightbulb went off in his head. "Thank you, Mr. Box. It looks like we need to pay another visit to Miss Morrall."

"She left work." Box stood and shook their hands, slipping a piece of paper into Linn's. "My guess is she's headed home to pack. She was very skittish after y'all left."

"Why did you hold onto the lipsticks?"

He exhaled sharply. "I wanted to make sure I had a reason to meet with you. When I discovered that this company makes customized makeup, I knew it was information you needed."

"Let's go." Linn dashed to her car, pocketing the lipsticks. In the car, she dropped them into a paper bag Steve pulled from the glove compartment.

He slapped their police light on top of the car. "Siren?"

"No, let's surprise her." Linn grinned and sped toward the address Box had given her.

~

"Relax, Sharon." Meaghan leaned back on her pile of bedpillows and crossed her legs. A fun night with sweet Lance had left her exhausted. Now, the dear young man snored next to her, his hands handcuffed to the bed's headboard. She'd have to take him back to the basement eventually. Her pets needed feeding.

She probably should have killed her cousin the moment she saw Meaghan dragging Bill Nelson into her house that first day. Sharon hadn't thought much about it until the news said he'd disappeared, then he'd escaped. But she was family. "I trust you kept your mouth shut."

"Of course." Her voice shook. "I need to come stay with you. I can't go back to work. My nerves will give everything away."

"Don't you dare come here," Meaghan hissed. "You might be followed. Go to Uncle Dan's cabin. Grandma's house is mine."

"I can't stay at the home of the man who molested me. Even you can't be that cruel."

"Can't I?" Meaghan ran her fingers through Lance's hair. "Fine. I could use help with my…guests. Don't come here, though. Wait for me in back of the supermarket in two hours. I'll come and get you. Do not be seen." She clicked off her phone. Having Sharon where she could keep an eye on her might be a good thing.

~

Linn stared through the car's windshield at the small cottage-style home. "It doesn't look like anyone's here."

"My guess is, she's flown the coop." Steve shoved his door open and exited the car.

"Be careful. You know what happened the last time officers approached a house." Linn stepped to his side, one hand resting on the butt of her gun.

"We aren't going to open any doors." Steve moved to the empty carport and peeked through a small window into the kitchen. "It's dark."

Linn glanced in, taking in the sink empty of dishes, the spotless counters, and a red light on the coffee pot. She smiled. "She's either here or just left because she prepared coffee." She slowly turned the door handle.

When they didn't blow up, she pushed the door open. "Police."

No shouts or gunshots welcomed them. Linn stepped inside and headed to the right while Steve went to the left.

No one was in the bathroom. "Clear."

"Dining room clear."

The next room was a bedroom where it was obvious someone had left in a hurry. The closet door hung open. Clothes were scattered across the bed and on the floor. The dresser drawers wouldn't shut because of clothes not put away properly. "In here," Linn called.

Steve joined her and frowned. "We just missed her."

Linn nodded. "Let's talk to Drew about a chopper."

The ride back to the station was silent as Linn sorted through the information in her head. They knew who the killer was, they strongly suspected the men she'd taken were still alive, but they had no idea where they were being kept. How long would someone as criminally minded as Meaghan keep them alive?

She parked near the entrance and made a beeline for the conference room. A handsome Asian man got to his feet when she entered.

"Detective McFarland, I presume. I'm Agent Chang." He held out his hand. "It's nice to meet you."

"Likewise." She sat next to Drew, catching sight of the papers in front of him. "What are you working on?"

"You aren't going to like it," Agent Mayne said, entering the room with a tray full of coffee cups.

"Tell me." Linn had a suspicious feeling it involved the handsome new agent.

"Chang came up with the wonderful idea of using ourselves as—"

"No." She crossed her arms and glared at the new agent, then transferred her attention to Mayne. "Surely you aren't in agreement."

"I'm not." She handed Linn a Styrofoam cup of coffee.

"It makes sense, Detective." Chang twirled an ink pen between his fingers. "We've come to the conclusion that Queen Coral is collecting men of different ethnicities. She doesn't have an Asian that we know of. Plus, she's after the chief. Get her to take both of us and we're in."

"She's violent and unpredictable." Linn shook her head. "There has to be another way. Tell them, Steve."

He sighed. "I agree with them. We have to take her off the streets, and this may be the only way to do so."

"How can you say that?" Linn frowned. "You were

captured by a madman a few months ago and almost died. Then, you dated this…woman. Drew did die when that house blew up, and we lost an agent. I'm not going to lose Drew again."

"Then I'm going to have to release you from duty." Drew folded his hands on the table and fixed his eyes on her. "If you cannot be professional and take our relationship out of the equation, I have to remove you from the case."

"You don't have enough manpower as it is." How could he threaten her this way? "You'd do the same if the roles were reversed."

"Can you or can you not remain professional?"

"Fine." She grabbed her cup of coffee, knowing full well she wasn't acting anywhere close to a detective. "You can sleep in the spare room. No mixing work with pleasure." It didn't feel as good to toss the words he'd told her months before back into his face.

Drew's expression let her know in no uncertain terms how he felt about the way she was acting. As if she were a child that needed dismissed, he turned to Agent Chang. "As I was saying…we can't be together when she takes us. This will take two separate baits."

"This could take longer than those men have," Steve said. "I could hold a press conference taunting her. Since I dated her, she might respond to some of the more personal details of our relationship."

"Or she might just shoot you outright." Linn had had enough. She slammed her palms on the table and pushed to her feet. "I'll go along with whatever you…men decide. All I ask is that you look at every possible scenario. If Queen Coral is anywhere near as clever as The Photographer was, your idea is nothing more than a suicide mission."

# Chapter Sixteen

Linn picked at her hamburger, trying not to stare at Drew, deep in conversation with Agent Chang. She'd almost died at the hands of The Photographer. So had Steve. Now, Drew expected her to sit back while one of the most ruthless killers they've ever stalked takes him to her lair?

Yes, Linn was a detective. A damn good one, too. But this was the man she loved. Things were not the same.

"I'm going to the gym."

Steve glanced up, his brow furrowed. "When was the last time you did that?"

"I'm overdue." A fast speed on the treadmill or a bout with a punching bag ought to put her in a better mood. "Anyone want to join me?"

Drew barely turned his head and shook it no. The two agents also said no.

"I'll go." Steve closed his laptop. "Maybe a workout will clear my head."

Once they were headed to the gym, he said, "What's got you all worked up?"

"This stupid baiting idea. Someone is going to die." She

pulled into a parking space and cut the engine. "You and I have been too close to evil."

"Drew has too. He's told us about some of the cases he worked before meeting you."

She sighed. "I'm scared."

He put his hand on her shoulder. "Good. That'll keep you alert. Drew is a smart man. He's good at what he does. Let him do it."

"If it were anyone else but him." She shoved open her door and slid from the car.

In the dressing room, she donned workout clothes that should have been washed a month ago when she'd worn them. She tied her hair back in a ponytail and headed for the punching bag.

Steve leaned against the wall. "Want to spar with a live person?"

"I might hurt you." She tugged on her gloves.

He grinned. "I'll try to keep it easy for you."

"Ha ha." She stepped onto the mat and put her hands up. "What are the rules?"

"There are no rules." Steve stepped back, and Drew took his place.

"Traitor."

Steve smiled, waved, and headed for the weight machine.

Drew gave her a crooked smile. "I think you need to pummel me a bit."

"Are you recovered—" She snapped her mouth closed at the hard glint in his eyes. She'd keep her punches at his mid-section.

He bounced lightly on his feet. "Now's your opportunity to let loose some of the aggression you're feeling."

"I'm not," she jabbed, catching him in the ribs, "feeling aggression. I'm frustrated." Ow. He tapped her jaw.

"Don't lie." He tapped her again, a little harder.

"Stop hitting me in the face."

"It's just a love tap." His lips curled, and he danced around her. "Hit me."

She swung wild, missing.

His punch hit her in the gut, knocking the breath from her lungs. She ducked, bringing up her right hook, grinning at the grunt he gave when she connected.

She didn't know how long they danced and punched. Only that by the time they'd finished, she was panting and sweating heavily. She stood, arms hanging loose at her sides and met Drew's gaze. "I'm sorry for acting the way I did."

He pulled off his right glove and cupped her cheek. "Sweetheart, I can relate. But we joined this profession to save lives. To help people. I can't do that sitting behind a desk."

Swiping her arm across her eyes to wipe away the sweat, she nodded. "I know. This whole case has me off kilter. Sparring helped. Thanks."

He pulled her close, resting his chin on her head. "Don't ever apologize for loving me."

He smelled like a man who had worked out. His skin glistened. His shirt stuck to his chest. She wrapped her arms around his waist and hugged him tighter. Her man was smelly, sweaty, and very much alive. For that she was grateful.

"Let's hit the showers and get back to work with clear heads," Drew said, tilting her face up for a kiss.

~

Would you look at that. Meaghan lowered her binoculars. She'd followed Steve and the other detective to the gym and almost shouted with joy when the other two men she wanted strolled through the doors. Unfortunately, there was strength in numbers. In a confrontation, five law-enforcement people would win out over one woman no matter how clever she might be.

She raised the binoculars again. How does one catch a fish when the fish knows you're hunting it? With an irresistible lure. Hmm. She had some creative thinking to do.

As the agents and detectives filed out of the gym, she let her gaze linger for a few minutes on Steve. Perhaps if they'd met in a different time, before life had turned her upside down and shaken all the good out, they might have been able to have something special. Now, she'd catch him, keep him, and maybe, just maybe, he would be the one she released alive.

She placed her palm to the front windshield as if he could see her. Perhaps he could sense her.

Steve stopped and glanced around the parking lot before jogging to catch up with his partner. Meaghan would be jealous if she didn't know the blonde only had eyes for the chief.

She drove from the lot and headed up the mountain.

When she arrived home, she found Sharon in the basement with Meaghan's toys, feeding them, of all things. "What are you doing?" She slapped a fork out of her cousin's hands.

"I was lonely." Sharon retrieved the fork and wiped it on a napkin. "I can help you. I asked the big guy," she pointed at Jamal, "if he was hungry and he nodded. Wow, Meaghan. I had no idea of your collection. Can I have one?"

Meaghan narrowed her eyes. "They're mine."

"Can I get my own?"

"Seriously, Sharon. Look at you and look at me. Do you honestly believe that men like these will take a second look at pudgy little you?"

"There's no need to be mean." She picked up the plate. "I don't need someone as fine as these. I just need…someone."

This was getting out of hand. "You can feed them, you

can talk to them, but you can't play with them." Meaghan trailed her fingers across David Hernadez's naked chest. "I choose you tonight."

"Please. I don't even have to keep him down here with yours." Sharon's whiny voice was giving her a headache.

"You won't be able to. I'll have to help you."

Sharon clapped. "Where shall we go?"

Who knew Meaghan's proper cousin was as deranged as she was? She laughed. Maybe it ran in the family. "We'll go a seedy bar. You'll find someone good enough."

She sliced the zip tie around David's wrists. "Come on, handsome. You need a shower. Sharon, we need another case of zip ties."

"I'll head to the hardware store right now." She raced up the stairs.

~

Two hours later, they were no closer to knowing their next step. Linn twirled her water glass in the condensation on the table. "I hate to be a pessimist, but what if this is one case we can't solve?"

"We'll solve it." Drew breathed deeply through his nose. They had to. He was putting his and Chang's lives on the line. It had to work. If not…he glanced at those around the table…Steve would take care of Linn. He'd loved her before Drew came along.

"Chief?" Allie poked her head into the conference room. "We have another missing man. This time from a bar on the outskirts of town." She glanced at the paper in her hand. "Mack's."

He glanced at Linn. "That isn't even close to Meaghan's style of hunting grounds."

"Maybe she's getting desperate," Chang said. "If you want to check it out, Agent Mayne and I will stay here and go over the caseboard…again. We have to be missing something."

"Or Queen Coral really is that good." Mayne stood in

front of the board. "See y'all later."

Drew led Linn and Steve to an undercover squad car. "We stay together. It isn't time for her to pounce. It has to be on our terms."

"Got it." Linn hooked her seatbelt.

"I think he was talking to me." Steve tapped her on the shoulder before settling into the back seat. "You aren't exactly Meaghan's taste."

"Everyone's a comedian."

Drew laughed. They were silent on the drive to Macks. Drew parked in front of a wooden building that might have actually been painted a barn red once. Now the paint looked more like a leper's skin peeling. This was definitely not Meaghan's normal hunting ground.

He watched as mostly middle-aged men shuffled in and out. Occasionally, a younger man, clearly suffering from some form of addiction joined the mindless procession in and out of the bar. It didn't make sense.

"Let's go." He exited the car.

With Linn between them, they entered the dim recesses of the building and headed straight for a wooden bar marred with cigarette burns and knife gouges. Drew flipped open his badge. "Mind if we ask you a few questions?"

"Go ahead. It's a free country."

"Have you ever seen either of these women?" Linn laid a photo of Meaghan and one of Sharon on the scarred surface.

"Yeah, just a few hours ago. I thought it strange that a looker like that would come in." He rubbed his bald head.

"Did they talk to anyone?" Drew asked.

"The pretty one scoped out the room. She sat on that stool right there. Every man in the place was drooling when she crossed them long legs of hers. Then, she sent her friend, cute but a little chubby, over to talk to a man sitting in that booth." He pointed to a nearby table. "Then, the three of them left together. It was like the chubby gal was doing the work for Miss Gorgeous. All that one had to do was crook her finger."

Drew glanced at Linn, then back to the bartender. "What did this man look like?"

"He's a regular. Dark hair, skinny, around thirty-five years old. His name is Martin Dodge."

Steve wrote the name down. "Was he what you would consider handsome?"

"No, but he wasn't butt-ass ugly either. Just an ordinary man out for a drink after work. Has a wife and two kids. I think they're having problems in their marriage. He's never once left with a woman before."

Drew shrugged. The poor fool had never had one like Meaghan show interest in him before. He pulled a business card from inside his suit jacket. "Give us a call if you think of anything else."

"Wait a minute." The bartender's eyes widened. "You think that woman was Queen Coral? Do you think she took Martin? Man," he rubbed his head again, "I should have paid more attention."

"Sir, her photo has been plastered all over the news for days." Linn looked disgusted.

"I just got back from vacation in Mexico and heard about the disappearances last night. I'm sorry." His shoulders slumped. "I really hope Martin will be okay."

So did Drew. Outside, he turned to the others. "Martin isn't for Meaghan. He's for Sharon. They are definitely together."

What would happen now between the cousins? Were they both going to become collectors?

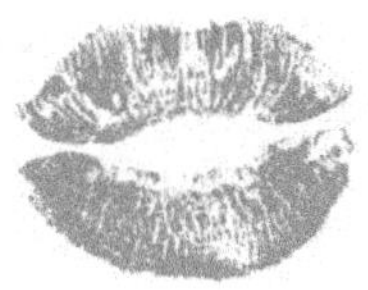

# Chapter Seventeen

Steve stood behind the podium, a sea of news reporters waiting for a press release. Linn still didn't like the idea of goading Queen Coral into taking one of the men she cared about, but she'd agreed to keep her thoughts to herself.

"The FBI has asked me to address the city in regards to the crimes committed by Meaghan Larson aka Queen Coral." Steve glanced at his notes. "Another man disappeared yesterday, Martin Dodge. We believe he was taken by Sharon Morrall, Larson's cousin. The women are believed to be working together at this point."

"Any more deaths?" A reporter asked.

"Not since Bill Nelson." Steve gripped the podium with both hands.

It should have been Linn up there. She didn't mind being in front of a crowd. Steve did.

"Why do you believe Queen Coral is no longer working alone?" Alan Barker, the favorite reporter of Upton Falls, asked.

Steve took a deep breath and stared into the nearest television camera. "We believe Larson has lost her nerve and can no longer continue her collection without help. If you have any information or have seen this woman, please call the number at the bottom of your screen. No more questions. Thank you." He left, taking his notes with him.

Linn watched as the reporters quickly scribbled down what little information Steve had given them. There would be many different versions of the same thing on the various news channels, but all of them would reiterate that Queen Coral was becoming inept.

That ought to draw her out of the woodwork. God help them all.

"What's next?" she asked, taking her seat in the conference room.

"Except for you and Agent Mayne, we three will start patrolling alone." Drew met her gaze. "Normally, that's a big no-no, but for this plan to work, she has to take us."

Linn knew that, she did, but it didn't stop her heart from dropping. She wanted to tell him that he didn't know what Meaghan did to the men she took. What if she forced him to have sex? Would he? If it kept him alive, she prayed he would. To stay alive he'd have to push his morals aside and do whatever it took. "This could take a while. You'll have to form a new routine and make yourselves accessible."

"Which means, I'm sending you away on assignment tomorrow night. I'll be home alone. Hopefully, she'll come then. You'll stay away until she does."

"Drew, I don't think—"

"The house is the easiest place for her to take me."

"I'll frequent the country club," Steve said, "making sure I leave late and appear drunk. If I go every Tuesday and Thursday, she's bound to think it's a pattern."

Chang sat silent for a moment. "I shouldn't be too difficult. I've been living in a hotel since I got here. Maybe she's stopped because of the pressure."

"Not a chance." Drew shook his head. "I've seen too

many egotistical killers to think she has. No, she enjoys the hunt as much as the domination."

Linn grabbed a bottle of water from the center of the table. Anything to keep her from begging Drew not to put himself as bait. She twisted off the cap and lifted the bottle to her lips, taking a sip. "Instead of sending me away, why not search on foot through the woods on the mountain? It worked for The Photographer. After a day or two of stomping around up there, she's bound to notice. It wouldn't be too hard for her to grab you if the closest searcher was five-hundred feet away." Her blood ran cold thinking of how close she'd come to dying in one of those silky red gowns The Photographer dressed his victims in.

Obsessed with her, he'd taken anyone who remotely looked like her. She rubbed the scar on her lip. The reason he'd waited so long to take her was because she hadn't been perfect.

Her skin crawled remembering the first time she'd met him when she'd been an exotic dancer to pay her way through school. The Photographer had taken advantage of her car running out of gas and raped her. That was the first step in his obsession.

"Linn?" Drew's voice pulled her out of her memory. "Are you listening?"

"Sorry." She set the bottle down.

"We're going to start searching at daylight tomorrow. I'd like you in the chopper with Mayne, while the three of us search on foot. Give us a heads up if you see anything suspicious."

"Okay." She'd definitely be keeping a close eye on him. From the air, she wouldn't be able to stop his abduction, but she could possibly follow the crazy woman who wanted him. "If she takes one of you, what then? Will you do the same thing the next day in hopes she takes another? I wouldn't."

"Good point," Chang said. "Whoever is left will

continue to make themselves as vulnerable as possible."

"I think you should all wear a tracker. In your watch, button, somewhere," Mayne said. "Larson will most likely discover it, but it would give us a starting point to search for you. We cannot allow ourselves to forget how smart this woman is."

~

Maeghan couldn't take anymore of the simpering foolishness going on between her cousin and her "guest." The man didn't act as if he minded being Sharon's prisoner. Why should he? She doted on him, giggling when they went to her room. The whole thing was disgusting.

She picked at a cuticle. Her men didn't look at her with anything but fear. Oh, they were accommodating enough when taken upstairs, they couldn't help it, but even then, fear tainted their playtime. Steve would be different. Steve loved her. She'd seen it in his eyes.

All she needed to do was convince him to come with her. Did she even need to finish her collection? Take the chief? Yes, she wasn't one to leave anything unfinished. She'd finish the collection and turn them over to Sharon before leaving the country with Steve. It was the perfect plan.

She hissed as she pulled the cuticle and made it bleed. What if Steve didn't join her? What if she was all wrong about how he felt? She cursed and got to her feet. She'd stick to her original plan and see where things went from there.

"Sharon!"

Feet thundered up from the basement. "What? I'm feeding the men breakfast."

"Forget that. I need a plan, and it involves you."

"Can I turn on the TV? Judge Judy is on, and most of your planning is just you thinking out loud anyway. I rarely have any say."

Meaghan rolled her eyes. Such a simpleton. "Sure."

She watched in astonishment as the only man she'd come close to caring about betrayed her in front of the entire state, taunted her, made her less of a woman. That sealed everything. She would continue her collection and make them all pay. "Turn that off. That rubbish is why I rarely watch TV. We're going to focus now and put an end to all this. I'm tired of playing."

Her smile made her cousin flinch.

When she had her plan in place, she'd take out her anger on her pets downstairs. She rubbed her hands together. "Ready?"

~

The phone rang off the hook with nosy people wanting information and kooks who swore they'd seen Queen Coral everywhere from the library to the bus station to the homeless camp outside of town. Linn hung up on the last thrill seeker. "Not one lead worth pursuing."

"Everyone wants their piece of the limelight." Drew kissed the top of her head. "We're getting close. We'll get her."

Linn wished she had the same confidence. There were killers who escaped the clutches of law enforcement. Some were caught twenty years or more later. Meaghan Larson was one of the most difficult predators they'd ever hunted. She settled back in her chair and studied the list of calls that had come in. Someone had to have    "

"Detective?" Allie rang on the intercom. "Another call on line one. They asked for you specifically."

"Thank you." Linn picked up the receiver. "Detective McFarland, how may I help you?"

"This is Baker's Pharmacy." A man cleared his throat. "I think the woman you're looking for, the one who's killing those men, is in my store."

"What is she purchasing?"

"First aid supplies. Bandages, antibiotic cream, super glue, etc. I have her on film if you want to see. She's a regular, but until the press release this morning, I wasn't exactly sure who she was."

"Your address?" Linn scribbled it down and snapped her fingers at Steve. "We'll be there in fifteen minutes. Try and stall her."

"Shouldn't be too hard. She's waiting on a prescription."

"Thank you." She slammed down the phone and grabbed her holster. "We've got a strong lead." And a fear that one of Queen Coral's captives might need medical attention.

After letting Drew know their destination, Linn drove quickly without the siren to a shady part of town and parked a few stores away from the drugstore. She peered through the front window then, not spotting Meaghan, exited into the bright afternoon sunlight.

Curious onlookers stared as she and Steve marched, hands on the butt of their guns, toward the drugstore. One mother pulled her son into an alcove.

A woman wearing a pharmacist's jacket ran screaming from the drugstore. Blood stained the front of her coat. "She killed him." She gripped Steve's arms.

He set her aside. "Stay there."

With a glance at Linn, they rushed into the store and up to the pharmacy counter. Lying in a pool of blood, his throat slit, was the head pharmacist. Linn whirled, searching the store. Spotting a door with a keypad, she asked. "How did she get in there?"

"Jumped the counter most likely. She was athletic." He pointed to a set of double doors at the back of the store. "Let's go."

Guns at the ready, they pushed through the doors. They'd entered the storage area. To their right was a bathroom with the door propped open. To their left was a folding table with chairs, most likely set aside for staff breaks. In front of them were pallets piled with boxes. The delivery door hung open.

Linn kicked a chair. "She got away. Again." She gritted her teeth.

"At least we suspect she's staying somewhere close." Steve put his gun away. "Let's secure the scene, take care of the hysterical woman outside, then take a look at that recording."

Two hours later, they sat in front of a monitor and watched as Meaghan, plain as day in tight jeans and a thin tee-shirt approached the counter with a basket full of supplies. She spoke to the pharmacist, left the basket on the counter, then stepped back out of sight. Ten minutes later, the pharmacist dialed the phone. Seconds after he hung up, Meaghan vaulted over the counter and slit his throat. Grabbing the basket of supplies and a few bottles off a shelf of prescription medications, she climbed back over the counter and disappeared from view.

Linn sighed. "He should have been more careful about calling me. She must have heard the conversation. My bet is she'll pack up and move."

Steve shook his head. "Too difficult with five hostages. I think she believes she's safe where she is. There are a lot of empty buildings around here. Most of them still have water and electricity. Forget the mountain, Linn. She's here in the city."

Hiding in the concrete jungle. Great. Linn preferred the woods where the closest hiding places were miles apart and scarce. Here…they'd search for weeks. "Let's talk to Drew. I'm sure he'll want to start with the buildings that still have utilities."

"How's he doing?"

"Drew?" She glanced sideways at Steve as they headed for her car. "Better. He still sleeps eight hours, unusual for him, but he has more energy in the morning. Why?"

"I'm only making sure he's physically up to the challenge ahead of him."

She gripped his arm. "If you're there…with him…please do what you can to keep him alive."

"I'd like to think we'd help each other." A shadow passed over his eyes. "I'll do my best."

She stared into the eyes of the man who had loved her first. She knew without a doubt that Steve would put his safety aside if it meant keeping Linn happy. Guilt raced through her veins. How much longer could she take advantage of his love before he started to resent her?

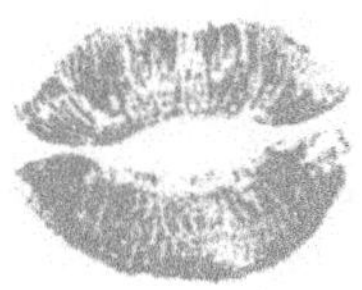

# Chapter Eighteen

A group of law enforcement officers, some borrowed from Little Rock, converged on the east side of town. Dressed in riot gear, with a SWAT team waiting, they were ready to hunt down a killer.

Drew reached over and squeezed Linn's hand. They'd had a long talk the night before about how she had to step down if he were taken. Because of that, he was partnering her with Mayne instead of himself. Drew would hunt with a rookie at his side, as would Steve and Chang.

"I love you," she said, not looking at him. She slipped her hand free and joined Agent Mayne on the edge of the search party.

He'd never felt more alone in his life.

"You ready for this?" Chang stepped beside him.

"As ready as I can be." Drew stared down the street, vacant except for a few obstinate young men who refused to be intimidated by the show of force. "It's possible she'll kill us outright. She may not be taking anyone anymore."

"I've thought that, too. No way to know." He clapped Drew on the shoulder. "Good luck."

"Same to you." With one last glance to where Linn stood, Drew followed the rookie to the building they'd been assigned to search. Just because Meaghan frequented Baker's Drugs didn't mean she lived in the neighborhood, but it was a good place to start their search.

Both men clicked on small flashlights and entered the building. Boards covered broken windows. Rat droppings littered the floor. Drew couldn't imagine Meaghan being caught dead in such a place, but if the building had a basement, perhaps she'd turned it into a home…of sorts.

Their footsteps kicked up dirt and thudded faintly on the concrete floor. Faded and chipped linoleum still clung to some areas with a last-ditch effort to stay.

Drew motioned with his hand for Rookie Orson to take one side of the hall, while he took another. The man nodded.

The first door squeaked as Drew pushed it open. He glanced around the small apartment, then into the tiny bathroom. Clear. The place had been vacant for a long time. All the bottom-floor apartments were the same. Uninhabited except for vermin.

"There's a basement," Orson whispered.

"Let's go." Drew led the way down a set of rickety, metal stairs. He kept a firm grip on the handrail, fearing any minute that the whole thing would collapse into the cavern below. He couldn't see anyone using the stairs on a regular basis.

As suspected the basement was empty. Two hours later they'd combed the entire building and came up empty. "Building one cleared," Drew said into his radio.

"Building two cleared," Steve said.

"Three cleared," Chang answered.

"Four cleared," Linn said.

"Onto the next," Drew ordered. "We don't stop until this entire neighborhood has been searched."

Drew made his way to the next building assigned to

him and Orson. It was clear before they stepped inside that someone had been in and out on a regular basis.

A gunshot sounded, then nothing. "Roll call," he said into his radio.

Everyone responded with an affirmative.

With his hand on his gun, he pushed open the door. He held up his fist for Orson to stop, listened, then motioned for the other man to go to the right.

A scuffling sound down the hall brought them together again. Crouched, guns at the ready, Drew led Orson to the last room on the right.

The door was open just enough to peer into a vagrant's paradise. A tattered sleeping bag lay spread in one corner. A battered TV tray, the kind used in the 1950s, stood in front of a three-legged stool. A candle burned from a chipped saucer. A man, his back to them, hunched over a small barbeque grill.

"Police." Drew called.

The man shrieked and jumped. His foot caught the grill. Hot coals spilled across the sleeping bag, catching it on fire.

Drew leaped forward, stomping out the flickering flames. He now owed a homeless man a new sleeping bag. "Sorry about that. I'll replace it."

The man glowered from under a head of matted hair. His mouth was barely discernible in a stained beard. "I ain't done nothing wrong."

"Vagrancy is a crime."

"I ain't hurting nobody."

Drew put his gun away. "I might be willing to overlook your squatting here if you'll answer a few questions."

The man frowned. "Why is the chief of police pounding the pavements? Shouldn't you be behind a desk?"

"Not this time. We're looking for a woman."

The man cackled, perching on the three-legged stool. "Ain't we all?"

"Queen Coral." Drew fished a photo of Meaghan from his pocket. "Have you heard of her?"

"Yep. She's the one taking all those men. I've seen her too."

Drew glanced at Orson, then back at the old man. "Where?"

"Here and there. She looks different sometimes, wearing disguises, but a woman like her sticks out. Even when dressed as a homeless woman."

"Do you know where she is now?"

He shook his head. "Nope. Don't reckon she'll come around here no more now that you're here. She used to shop at that corner market for food."

"Did she drive here?"

He shrugged. "I only seen a van once. One of them white-paneled things. Why is it killers always use panel vans?"

"I don't know."

The man sighed. "Other times, I seen her coming and going west of here. That's all I know."

"Thank you." Drew handed him a business card. "Please call if you think of anything. I'll have you a new sleeping bag delivered by tonight."

"You ain't kicking me out?"

"Not this time." He didn't have a problem with a harmless old man taking refuge in an empty building. Since he hadn't seen any signs of drug use, he'd let the man be.

He looked at Orson. "Let's head west.

~

There he is. Meaghan smiled and ducked back around the corner. The Asian was even more beautiful close up. Of course, all these toys were just…things…to occupy her time until she had Steve. Too bad he wasn't the one searching this particular building.

Fools. All of them. Did they honestly think she'd live in this squalor? Of course, the building she lived in wasn't a whole lot better, but at least it was a house.

She pulled her Glock from the pocket of her jacket and a syringe from the other. This was too easy. She was a ghost. In the paper shoes she wore, she barely left a footprint in the dust on the floor.

A whiff of cologne reached her. Something woodsy and masculine. The man even smelled heavenly. She couldn't wait any longer. She ran on her tiptoes, plunging the syringe into her prey's neck and shooting the other man. Yes, too easy.

~

Steve was starting to think the whole search was a waste of valuable time. Other than arresting a group of young men snorting coke in the bathroom of one of the buildings, he hadn't seen anyone other than the man he was partnered with. Who, he might add, was a poor excuse for an officer.

In one building, a rat had scampered across their path and the man almost shot himself in the foot. Now, he followed so close behind Steve that if he stopped suddenly his partner would run into him. He missed working with Linn.

"What was that?" Rookie Jones stopped. "A rat?"

"Most likely." They hadn't seen footprints of any other living thing. "There's no one here." As this was their last building, there was nothing to do but head back and wait for the others to join them.

Linn and Mayne were already back at the cars, cups of coffee in hand. "We came up empty."

"Yeah, us to." Steve grabbed one of the cups sitting on the hood of an SUV. "Other than some sick kids snorting coke off a toilet seat in a desperate need of cleaning, we didn't see any signs of life. Why haven't these buildings been torn down?"

Linn shrugged. "Last I heard they were going to renovate for low-income housing. That was two years ago."

They all jerked as a gunshot rang out.

"What direction did it come from?" Steve stepped away from the vehicle. Sound was hard to pinpoint on the street of brick buildings.

Linn unclipped her radio. "Roll call."

Everyone confirmed except for Chang.

"Chang?" Drew's voice carried a hint of alarm. "Anyone seen him or his partner?"

"No," Linn answered.

"The search has changed. Spread out and find signs of them."

With twenty law-enforcement officers and a SWAT team at the ready, Meaghan had still managed to sneak in and take one of them. Of course, they had no proof it was her, but Steve would bet everything he had that it was.

The sound of pounding feet rang out as everyone dispersed. Steve left Rookie Jones to go with someone else and joined Linn and Mayne as they headed for the end of the street.

Curious onlookers were emerging from the storefronts and scattered apartment buildings still being used. Steve waved them back. Curiousity had caused more collateral damage during his career than he cared to admit. What was it about people that drew them to witness danger and put themselves in harm's way.

Slowing their pace, the three entered the last building assigned to Chang. Steve glimpsed Drew running up to them as he pushed open the door. The sound of an engine coming to life roared down the hall. "She's getting away!"

He leaped over the body of an officer and barged out the back door into the alley. A white van careened around the corner of the building. Steve raced after it, taking a short cut between two buildings.

When he emerged on the other side, he spotted the van turning another corner.

"Where?" Linn and Drew joined him.

"That way."

They spread out, dodging cars and sightseers.

Steve leaped over a chain-link fence as the van sped down another alley. A pitbull lunged toward him. Heart in his throat, Steve grappled for the fence and got himself over as the dog's teeth clamped onto the hem of his pants. Leaving a piece of fabric behind, he continued the chase, yelling into his radio.

"Suspect leaving alley and emerging onto Third Street. We need roadblocks. Now!"

"White van drove onto sidewalk," Drew said. "Several bystanders injured. Van heading for Second Street."

Steve's breath came in gasps as he rejoined Linn at the end of the alley. Without speaking, they cut through an unfenced yard toward Second Street, where they met up with Drew. The three continued down an alley of small shops.

The van emerged at the end, facing them, then sped toward them.

Steve caught a glimpse of Meaghan's grinning face as she blew him a kiss before he leaped out of the way. He landed on top of several black bags full of garbage. Scrambling to his feet, he planted his feet firmly on the gravel of the alley and fired at the van, his shots joining those of Drew and Linn's.

The van continued on its way, the back of it riddled with bullet holes.

Steve's shoulders slumped. "She got away. With Chang."

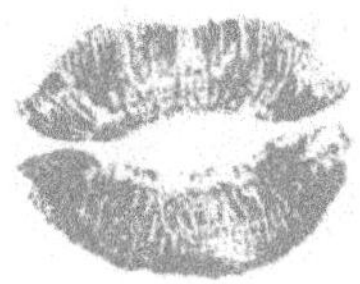

# Chapter Nineteen

"Hello, handsome." Meaghan stretched as she stood from the tattered lounge chair she kept in the basement. It was about time Agent Chang opened his eyes. Oh, yes, she knew his name. She'd gone through his wallet while stripping him to his underwear. "I do believe you were looking for me."

He muttered something under the gag in his mouth.

"Darling, I can't hear you." She removed the gag. "What was that?"

"They'll be looking for me."

"Will they?" She grabbed his watch from a nearby table and dangled it in front of him. "I've removed the tracking device. Did you think me stupid?"

"The opposite, in fact."

"Hmmm." She trailed her hand across his chest and around his back. "You are a fine specimen. Too bad you aren't what my heart wants. Shocked to know I'm capable of feelings?" She laughed. "While I do enjoy my little collection and the fun it brings, it's Steve I really want. Right here by my side where he belongs."

"Let me call him. He'll come if it means releasing these men."

"Oh, honey. I'm not finished yet. Before I have Steve, I need that gorgeous chief of police."

"Why?" Chang narrowed his eyes. "Why take us if you only want one man?"

She leaned so close she could see her reflection in his dark eyes. "Because men are pigs, good for one thing and one thing only. When I tire of you, I kill you and rid the world of one more handsome man who thinks he's a god, worthy of every woman's desire."

"We aren't all like that."

"Possibly, but I've not met but one man who makes me think different. Look around you, Agent. Each of these lovely specimens were picked up by hoping to have sex with me. It never occurred to them I'd say no. Now, they've had their fun and will eventually lose their life because of it." She laughed as the men groaned.

She jerked one shoulder, then returned to lounge. "Quiet now. I've plans to make. See how the others remain silent unless spoken to? That's how you must be if you don't want the gag." She smiled. Oh, yes, she had plans to make. Grand plans.

~

Drew stared out the kitchen window, sipping a cup of hot coffee as the sun came up. When he'd spotted the young police officer dead in a pool of blood, it reinforced the fact that more people would die while they fought to bring down Queen Coral.

Was Chang being tortured? Was he already dead? Drew's hand shook as he set the empty cup in the sink. For all his bravado he was terrified. Coming as close to death as he had, left a trickle of fear running through him. Not that the fear would keep him from doing his job, but only that he was a different man than before. Less self-assured. More aware of his mortality.

Linn wrapped her arms around his waist and hugged him from behind. "You're awfully deep in thought so early."

"Just thinking about Chang." He turned to face her, wrapping his arms around her. "Also mentally preparing myself to search another neighborhood."

"This one is occupied. The residents won't appreciate us traipsing in and out of their homes."

"Nope." He tilted her face up for a kiss. "I'd better not find out someone is hiding Meaghan's whereabouts."

"Why would they? Everyone has to know by now how dangerous she is."

"Some people hate the law more." He gave her another kiss, then stepped back. "Ready?"

"No." Her gaze searched his. "Today might be the day I lose you."

"You could never lose me, sweetheart. Even if God takes me home, I'll live right here." He laid his hand over her heart. "And here." He kissed her forehead.

She gave a sad smile. "I'd rather have you right here." She wrapped her arms around him again and squeezed before letting go. "Let's catch this woman."

Two hours later, along with another large group of law enforcement officers, they marched up and down residential streets, knocking on doors and searching the buildings. If no one was home, they found a way in. If someone objected, they searched on the exception of an emergency. Sooner or later, Queen Coral would run out of places to hide.

Drew glanced to where Linn and Mayne entered a liquor store before he opened the gate of a rundown duplex. A small courtyard with cracked bricks and weeds growing through whatever hole they could find gave a sad welcome to anyone entering.

Because he didn't want another police officer to die, Drew had elected to search alone that day and give

Meaghan a better chance of spotting him. He had no doubt she was hunting him. Sometime that afternoon, he'd come face to face with her.

He knocked on apartment number one.

An elderly woman opened the door. "I was expecting you."

"You were?"

She nodded. "You're looking for my daughter."

Drew stared at her for a moment, seeing a similarity in the eyes and shape of the nose. "Excuse me?"

"Queen Coral, Meaghan Larson, whatever name you want to call her is my daughter. Please, come in."

"Ma'am." Drew entered the clean but minimally furnished apartment. "If she's your daughter, why haven't you come forward?"

"I enjoy breathing." She sighed. "Sit. Let me tell you about her. Perhaps it will help."

Drew perched on the edge of a leather chair. "Go on."

"Meaghan was molested by her uncle, repeatedly, if she's to be believed. At that time, I couldn't believe it. Refused to believe that my brother was doing to my daughter exactly what he'd once done to me. But rather than pick up the pieces of what was left of her soul and move on, my daughter chose to take it out on every man she met." She grabbed a tissue from a nearby box and dabbed her eyes. "By the time I admitted to the abuse, she'd gone. I haven't heard from her since. Imagine my surprise at seeing her face on the evening news."

"Imagine." This woman was almost as crazy as her daughter. What mother allows this to happen to her child and does nothing?

"I see your disgust on your face. You must realize how much abuse injures a woman."

"I'm trying to. Why would Meaghan take men?"

"It puts her in a position of power, I suppose. Gives her control. My brother was a very handsome man. He could have anyone he wanted, and did, including my little girl."

"Where is your brother now?"

"I killed him the day my daughter left my life. He's buried under the brick courtyard out front. I suppose you'll be taking me to jail now."

"Once we confirm your story, yes." Drew radioed for Allie to contact a construction crew. When he'd finished, he fixed his gaze on the woman in front of him. "Do you have any idea where Meaghan might be keeping these men?"

"Her uncle owns a house on a few acres just outside of town. Well, I suppose it belongs to me now, since I'm his only living relative other than Meaghan. My guess is she's there."

"You suspected and said nothing while men were taken, tortured, and killed." He stood.

"My dear officer. Have your forgotten I hate men as much as my daughter? The only difference is I chose to live alone with my hate." She waved a hand toward the door. "Go on. I'll wait for someone to come arrest me."

Drew offered her a business card, which she refused. Shaking his head, he stepped outside. Linn and Mayne were heading across the street to a video store. He closed the apartment door.

"Hello, gorgeous." Meaghan stepped from behind a rhododendron bush, put a finger to her lips, and pointed the gun at Linn.

Drew raised his hands, let the business card fluttering to the ground under a bush behind him.

~

"This is a total waste of time." Linn leaned against the brick wall of the video store and swiped her arm across the sweat beading on her brow.

"She's got to be somewhere," Mayne, ever the voice of reason, said. "People aren't invisible. We just haven't found the right person to ask yet."

Linn pushed away from the wall. "Then let's keep pounding the pavement."

Steve jogged across the street toward them. "Any luck?"

"Nope." Linn shook her head. "You?"

"She's been spotted a few times, but nothing in days." He handed her and Mayne each a bottle of water. "She knows this neighborhood very well." He raised his eyebrows. "One old lady said she grew up here, but then she started rambling on about little green men, so I'm not sure if her story is true." He twisted the cap off his bottle and guzzled it half gone.

"There might be some truth in that." Linn glanced around them. "She knows the area, she's been spotted several times, which leads me to believe she doesn't venture anywhere else much. Maybe she's closer than we think."

"Then we'll find her." He flashed a smile and strode down the sidewalk.

Linn wished she were as confident as everyone else. She scanned the street, looking for Drew. She hadn't caught a glimpse of him in over an hour. Worry crawled up her arm like baby spiders just hatched. No, she'd promised him she wouldn't dwell on what ifs, only on what she could see and do.

Just as she started to head down the sidewalk, several officers sprinted toward a duplex across the street. While she watched, a construction crew arrived and carried jack hammers into the courtyard. She cut Mayne a quick look. "Let's go."

They dashed across the street as the first deafening sound of a jackhammer against brick filled the air. Linn approached one of the officers. "What's going on?" She yelled.

"The chief phoned the precinct and said the woman inside claims she killed her brother and buried him here."

Linn figured she'd go talk to woman. She knocked several times before deciding the woman wouldn't answer. Gun drawn, she pushed the door open. Sitting upright on the sofa was an older version of Meaghan. In the center of the woman's forehead was a single gunshot wound.

She phoned for an ambulance before rejoining Mayne. "This has just become a crime scene." She explained about the body inside.

"Guess we wait," Mayne said.

It seemed an eternity by the time the ambulance arrived and the bricks broke into pieces. Then two men with shovels tackled the packed dirt.

Linn leaned over the hole. "What is that?"

"I think it was once a cardboard box." Mayne shuddered. "Not a fitting casket for anyone."

Pieces of a human skeleton lay at the bottom of the hole. Spying a wallet, Linn pulled a rubber glove from her pocket and picked it up. She flipped it open. "Belonged to a Hank Larson." She glanced at the duplex. "Any idea yet on the woman inside?"

"No one's looked. We've been focused on this."

Linn carried the wallet inside and studied the room. A rolltop desk set against one wall. She opened it to reveal several envelopes. The top one was addressed to Helen Larson. Husband and wife? Brother and sister? Meaghan's relatives?

She opened a drawer and pulled out a photo album. Inside were pictures of a cute child and milestones as that child grew. On the last page was a high school graduation photo of Meaghan Larson. Under the photo were the words "my beautiful daughter."

The dead woman was Meaghan's mother. The man in the yard had to be her uncle. Why had Helen killed her brother?

"Linn?" Mayne stepped into the apartment. "I found this under a bush." She held out Drew's business card. "It hasn't been there long."

Linn's heart plummeted to her feet. "Drew was here. Meaghan has him."

# Chapter Twenty

Linn paced in front of the conference table. "What is taking so long to get information on Hank Larson?"

"They're going as fast as they can." Steve's gaze followed her. He'd give anything to take away the pain she had to be feeling. Why hadn't Meaghan taken him? He'd done everything short of knocking on her door, which he would do if he knew where she was.

Linn whirled and glared at him and Mayne. "I can't just sit here and wait."

"You don't have a choice." Mayne met her stare. "I lost the man I loved, you might lose yours, but we have a job to do."

Linn's shoulders slumped. "You're right." She fell into a chair. "I'm not good with inactivity."

"Then let's go look for some clues." Steve stood. Regardless of whether they found anything, keeping Linn occupied would be good for all of them. "We'll start where the body was found and spread out from there. Meaghan can't live far. Chang and Drew were both large men."

"She had a van. Once they were inside, she could be

anywhere."

"No, she can't. She's too active here in town."

Linn nodded. "Let's go. Mayne?"

"I'm waiting for Chang's replacement." She sighed. "The precinct goes through borrowed FBI like a toddler with cheerios."

The ride back to the crime-scene, taped off duplex was made in silence. Several times Steve wanted to reach over and take Linn's hand. But, she wasn't his to console that way. Once Drew arrived on the scene last year, she'd made it very clear that hers and Steve's relationship was strictly platonic. Dare he have hope because they had yet to set a wedding date?

He knew Linn's past, first as an exotic dancer, then a rape victim, so he understood her reluctance to commit. Still, he couldn't help but wonder why she hadn't married Drew.

"Why so quiet?" She cut him a glance as if she knew he was thinking about her.

"Thinking about this crazy case."

"Remember your promise. You said you'd make sure Drew lived no matter what you had to do ."

"I remember." He shoved open his door and approached the hole in the courtyard.

"I'm going inside. I had to have missed something before."

No doubt. She'd been searching when Mayne showed her Drew's business card. "I'll look around out here."

Even as careful as the technicians had been, the ground was marred with multiple footprints. Steve stood and stared into the hole that had held a man's body for over ten years. The ME hadn't confirmed cause of death, but Steve had seen the bullet hole in the skull. A hole very similar, he was told, to the one in Mrs. Larson's head.

He turned and headed for the narrow alley behind the row of duplexes. Meaghan must have parked the van near the dumpster as evidenced by drag marks. He knew the woman was fit, but she was stronger than he'd thought to be able to drag men the size of Chang and Drew.

Tire tracks went in both directions, the gravel so bare in some parts, he couldn't tell which direction the van would have gone. Deciding it most likely headed forward rather than do a U-turn, he headed that way, stopping when the alley connected with the street.

Footsteps crunched behind him. He pulled his gun and spun. "Linn, I almost shot you."

She smiled. "You're a bit skittish for a man who wants to be taken."

"I need to be taken, not want. There's a big difference." He put his weapon away. "Find anything?"

"Nothing. The woman is a ghost. Other than the photo album, it's as if Helen Larson had forgotten she had a daughter."

"Mother was as crazy as her daughter."

~

Meaghan straddled Drew's lap and slapped his cheek until his beautiful blues opened. "Hello."

"Get off me."

She smirked. "Really? You want to take that attitude with the woman who can hurt you? Make you beg for death?" She picked up a scalpel from a nearby table. "I wouldn't want to mar your perfection, although I've noticed you carry a few scars." She lowered her head and claimed a kiss, shoving her tongue into his mouth, withdrawing at the first hint of a bite.

"You are a naughty one." She laughed and climbed off him. "I do believe you know Agent Chang."

"I do. What's your plan, Meaghan? Why take innocent men?"

Her eyes flashed. "There's no such thing. Only one man has ever treated me as something worthy."

"Steve Chavez." The woman's obsession with Linn's

partner could get them killed.

"Very smart, chief." She strolled away from him, the lacy one-piece leaving very little to the imagination. The woman knew her power over men. She sat on a lounge chair across from him, crossed her long legs, and fixed her dark eyes on his. She stared without speaking for so long, Drew started to fidget.

"Sharon." Meaghan yelled up the stairs. "Wine, please. Several bottles and glasses."

"Where's the man your cousin took?"

"Upstairs. Stupid fool doesn't mind being a kept man. My dear cousin doesn't even lock him up."

Why hadn't he released the prisoners? Drew glanced at the stairs.

"You're wondering why he doesn't help you?" Meaghan tilted her head. "Because if he does, I told him I'd kill his family. He's an only child, but dotes on his mother and father. Love is a powerful weapon, isn't it, chief?"

Sharon returned with a tray of glasses and wine bottles. "Pour us each a drink, please."

"Do you want me to help them drink it, too?" Sharon narrowed her eyes. "What's your purpose here?"

"It's a party." Meaghan swung her legs over the side of the lounge. "Don't you like a party? We're celebrating the final stages of my plan."

Drew sneaked a glance at Chang. A muscle ticked in the man's jaw. He seemed as nervous about this final stage as Drew did. Once Meaghan had Steve she'd have no use for the others. This they knew. What he didn't know was how to stop her.

After being force-fed wine, and Meaghan heading upstairs to get her "beauty rest," Drew fought against the zip ties on his hands. If he could get them under the chair and over his legs, he could find something to cut through them with. They were in a basement full of crates and boxes. There had to be something. What he wouldn't give to be double-jointed.

"We need to do something fast," Chang said.

"I agree."

"Don't talk." Jamal shook his head. "If she hears you, she comes down here and someone pays the price. I've scars to prove it." He showed cigarette burns on his torso.

"Who's her favorite?" Drew leaned forward and looked down the line of men.

"I am." A man in his early twenties answered. "I…respond…quicker." His face reddened.

"You're Lance. Okay." Drew gave a nod. "The next time she takes you upstairs, you have to act fast."

"She ties me to the bedpost."

"Then attack before that happens. Your hands may be tied, but you have your head and your legs."

Lance hung his head. "I'll try, but if I fail, she'll kill me." He glanced up from under his bangs. "Can you live with that?"

Drew sighed. "No." He'd have to find a way to have Meaghan take him upstairs. He would risk his life for the others without hesitation. "What do I do to get invited upstairs?"

"Just wait," David Hernandez said. "She always takes a man on the first night."

"She hasn't taken me up yet," Chang replied.

That wasn't good. If she were tiring of her game, they didn't have much time.

~

Meaghan poured herself another glass of wine. The men had drunk when the glass was lifted to their lips, each settling their gaze on her with each sip. How easy it was to make them behave. Too easy. Boring, really.

But, the chief and Chang? They were different. Those two still had fire. That's why she couldn't risk bringing them to her room. They'd fight her. The others were too frightened, enamored, whatever each of them saw in her, to put up much of a struggle.

It didn't matter. She'd use her newest toys to convince Steve to come to her.

She tapped her fingernail against her teeth. How? She could threaten Detective McFarland. The chief—Steve, too—would do anything to prevent her demise. Meaghan smiled. In the morning, she'd force the handsome chief to make a phone call. Right now, she'd send the detective a message.

She grabbed one of the many throw-away phones she'd purchased and sent the following text:

I'm enjoying the chief. What a gorgeous hunk of man flesh. The problem is I'm getting bored and need to do something to shake things up. Whatever will do?

She hit send and smashed the phone before turning off her bedroom light. Things were going to get interesting.

~

Linn glanced at the text. "Mayne, look at this." She showed the message to the agent who was spending the night at Linn's now that Drew was gone. They could both use the company and there was safety in numbers. Not that Linn expected anything from Meaghan but a bullet in the back. Instead, she got a text. "What do you think she means?"

"I don't think we'll be sitting around waiting for much of anything after tonight. She's going to make a big move soon."

Linn lowered herself to the sofa. "But what?" More deaths? More abductions? A bold move on Steve? Too many questions, too few answers.

"Why didn't you hook up with Steve?" Mayne sat on the other end of the sofa and propped her bare feet on the coffee table. "He's handsome, has those killer, light green eyes, and he's a rare gentleman."

"We're partners, and I met Drew." She sighed and rested her head against the sofa back. "Steve is like a brother. He's always been there for me. He'd do anything I asked. But, my heart never felt romantic toward him."

Mayne nodded. "It seems strange he hasn't married. I think the man still loves you."

Linn didn't think he did, she knew. "I know." She closed her eyes and thought of Drew.

Was he injured? Was Meaghan having "fun" with him? Her stomach lurched. She wouldn't blame him for his part in any of it. He'd promised to come back to her. She knew if it was in his power, he would.

"We'll find them, Linn." Mayne nudged Linn's leg with her foot.

"I hope so." She forwarded the text to Steve. Within seconds, her phone rang.

"When did you get this?"

"Ten minutes ago." Linn closed her eyes. "Any news?"

"Hank Larson died of a bullet to the head."

"Anyone know where he lived?"

"Not yet. Do I need to come over?"

Linn shook her head, even though he couldn't see her. "No, Mayne is here. We thought it best we stick together from here on out."

"I agree. Keep me posted if anything else comes up. I'm here."

"I know you are." She pressed off and reached for the glass of wine on the end table. "It's jobs like this one that make me question why I'm in law enforcement."

"Because you're good," Mayne said. "I read about The Photographer case. You're one tough cookie, Detective McFarland."

Linn grinned ironically. "It's easy when you're the one in danger."

"Drew was in agony worrying over you. Now you're in the same situation. He's one of a kind. He'll make it out of this."

The wine must be affecting her because Linn laughed.

"Drew has a way of charming a woman until she can't think straight. Maybe his charm will work on Meaghan."

"That would be sweet." Mayne lifted her glass in a toast. "To justice."

"To justice." Linn clinked her glass against the other woman's.

*Bring it on, Meaghan. Whatever you got.*

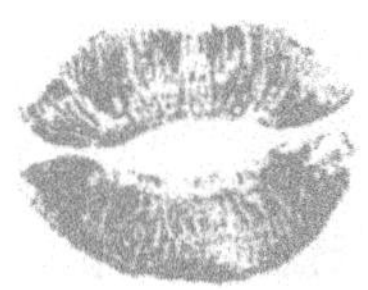

# Chapter Twenty-One

Meaghan stared at the men sitting in a straight row, all looking at her as if she were going to offer them a treat. All except for the chief and the agent. Those two still had defiance in their eyes.

It might be fun to break them. It wasn't time to implement the rest of her plan and complete her collection. First, Steve needed to sweat.

She unlocked a drawer in a file cabinet and withdrew a Beretta nine-millimeter. Keeping it aimed at Drew, she cut the zip ties binding the agent's hands and feet to the chair. "We're about to get better acquainted, Agent Chang." At his raised eyebrows, she continued, "I know your name because I looked in your wallet, silly."

She poked the gun in his back, guiding him to manacles attached to the concrete wall by chains. "I haven't had to use these on any of the others, but the hope in their eyes died much sooner than yours has. I think you need a little persuasion." If she made him scream enough, Chief Andrew Wayne might cow a little.

"Back against the wall, please. Any hesitation or

attempt to escape will result in the death of one of the others. Do you understand?"

He glanced over her shoulder, at Andrew, most likely, then nodded.

Meaghan sighed. She would definitely have to take care of Andrew. He thought he was running the show and needed to be taught who, exactly, was in control.

She secured Chang's hands in the manacles, then stepped back and studied the broad chest and chiseled stomach. "Yummy. It's almost a shame to scar that skin. How has an FBI agent managed to not have a single scar?" "When he didn't answer, she slapped him. "I asked you a question."

He frowned. "Lucky, I guess."

"Or perhaps you aren't as brave as you think you are." Oh, she would make him yell.

She trailed her fingers down the center of his chest, laughing as the muscles rippled under her touch. "Maybe I should take you upstairs first. You won't be very responsive when I've finished with you."

"You're not my type."

"Oh, really?" She set the gun on top of a nearby crate and uncapped a bottle of fingernail polish remover. "Very flammable." She poured the liquid down the crease of his chest, wiping it away before it soaked the waistband of his jockey shorts. "Wouldn't do to damage your goodies." She set the polish remover down and picked up a lighter.

She'd expected Agent Chang to ask her to stop before now. She ignited the lighter and held it up, watching the flicker of the flame in his dark eyes.

"Wait."

She let the flame die and turned to face Andrew. "Yes?"

~

"Don't do this." Drew swallowed past the lump clogging his throat. "What do you want? I can help you."

She tilted her head. "I told you. I want Steve."

"I can get him for you. There's no need to torture anyone."

"I'm not ready for Steve. You're friends, correct?"

Drew nodded.

"Then if he worries for a while, he'll be more compliant when he's in my hands."

"Not necessarily." Drew met Chang's gaze. From the determination on the other man's face, he knew something was working itself out in his mind. Drew gave a small shake of his head.

Chang sighed and lowered his head.

If the agent tried anything, Meaghan would definitely kill him and most likely the others. Since she seemed to have forgotten her game with the lighter, as long as Drew kept her attention on him, Chang could take it easy. If she turned back to finish the job, Drew wouldn't stop the man from trying to defend himself.

"Steve isn't an egotistical man," Drew said. "He's a gentleman, through and through. You won't have any trouble with him."

"I know he's a gentleman," she hissed. "That's why I want him. Men like you, and these," she waved her arm, "need to be taught a lesson."

"We aren't your uncle, Meaghan. Not one of us would dare treat a woman, much less a child, the way you and your mother were treated. She killed him, you know? Your mother killed your uncle years ago."

"Why?" She narrowed her eyes. "She didn't care a damn what happened to me."

"Obviously she cared a great deal. She buried his body under the brick courtyard after she killed him."

The information seemed to confuse her. She closed her eyes and stared at the floor. After a few minutes, she dashed up the stairs, slamming the basement door behind her.

"Man, she left me hanging," Chang said.

Drew laughed. "Better than what she did have planned for you. Is there any way out of those?"

Chang studied the manacles above his head. "Nope. What if you bust your chair? Can you get your hands free if you do that?"

"Are you two crazy?" David Hernandez frowned. "If you misbehave, she punishes you."

Drew rolled his eyes. "I'm not a child, and she's not my mother." He wrapped his hands around the spindle on the back of his chair and pushed to his feet. Now what? He couldn't very well walk if his feet were tied together. He hopped, barely moving two inches. This would take all day.

"Drop and break that chair," Chang said.

"If I hit my head, I might not regain consciousness for a while. I can't risk it." The knock he'd taken to the head during the explosion still kept him off kilter at times. When no one spoke up, he said, "Okay. I'll—"

"I'll do it." Jamal lunged to his feet, then fell backward before Drew had lowered his chair. He hit the floor with a thud and lay there gasping for air like a beached fish. "I'm…free. Now…what?"

"Find a way to cut through the zip ties."

He rolled into a ball and slipped his feet between his arms. After several attempts, he got to his feet and hopped to a small counter that looked as if it might hold some tools. "Oh, wow. She's got some wicked stuff here. I'm not so sure about this now. She could really put a hurt on me."

Drew should have chanced it. It was selfish of him to ask anyone to increase the danger to themselves.

Footsteps scuffed at the top of the stairs.

"Lie down," Drew whispered. "On top of the broken chair. Close your eyes. Quick, man. You fell and hit your head."

Jamal hopped, which would have been comical if they were in any other situation. As it was, Drew feared he wouldn't make it back before the door opened.

The door at the top of the stairs opened.

Jamal crumbled to the floor.

Sharon came down, a tray of cups and a pitcher of water in her hands. "Hello, oh, what happened?" She set the tray down and rushed to Jamal's side.

"The leg on his chair broke," Drew said. "He fell over and hit his head."

"Oh, Meaghan is going to be so mad." Sharon grabbed a folding chair from behind some boxes. When she turned, she spotted Chang. "What in the world is my cousin thinking?"

She grabbed the gun from the top of the crate. "No funny stuff." She unlocked the shackles on Chang's wrists. "Go sit back down."

Chang rotated his arms. "Thank you."

"I'm not a monster."

Once he was back in his chair, she used new zip ties to secure him. By now Jamal was pretending to wake up. "No wonder Meaghan needs my help. Taking care of all of you is a full-time job for one person."

"Not if you let us go," Chang said.

"I can't do that. You know what she's like when she's mad. Besides, I'm in this now." Sharon replaced the gun in the filing cabinet drawer, but didn't lock it. "Now, who's thirsty? Then, I'll have to help you relieve yourselves."

Drew almost choked. "What?"

"You didn't think she untied you so you could go to the bathroom, did you?" Sharon laughed. "Meaghan isn't very big. You could easily overtake her. But ask these other men what happens when she's mad."

"Where is she?"

"She ran out, shouting that she needed to verify some information." Sharon shrugged. "If she doesn't offer, I rarely ask."

As soon as Sharon had finished demoralizing them by

"helping" them relieve themselves, Drew glanced at the others. "Has she hurt all of you?"

Jamal nodded. "A cigarette on me. David has a strip of skin missing where she used a sharp cheese grater. Bill had it the worst, especially after he escaped."

"How did he escape?"

"I think she let him go as part of her game," Lance said. "I noticed you didn't mention me in your line of torture."

"You're her pet. The worst she does to you is take you to bed."

"You have no idea what she does to me up there. It's degrading."

"You don't seem to mind too much," David said. "You're such a good boy, you get out of here three or four times a week. Otherwise, she's down here bothering us. So, personally, I'm grateful for any time that insane woman isn't with us."

Chang cursed. "This isn't turning out as planned."

Drew wasn't giving up yet. He'd managed to distract her from torturing Chang, he'd figure something out to get her to release him. Then, he'd act, regardless of the consequences.

No more PTSD-like actions for him. If he died, so be it. It would be worth it if it saved the lives of the others. Linn would be okay. Steve would take good care of her.

~

Linn hit the punching bag as hard as she could, over and over, until her arms ached and her breath came in pants. What she wanted to do was pound the pavements, bang on doors, whatever it took to find Drew.

Steve insisted they wait, convinced Meaghan had yet to make her big move. When she did, he said, they'd catch her.

"Meaghan has been spotted at her mother's house." Steve wiped a hand towel across his face. "Let's go."

Nodding, excitement welling in her, Linn yanked off

the boxing gloves, grabbed her bag with her badge and gun, and raced to the parking lot. She had the engine started before Steve had his seatbelt fastened. "Call Mayne and hold on."

Tires squealed as she peeled from the parking lot. With siren screaming, they skid to a stop in front of Helen Larson's home. Standing in front of the hole in the courtyard stood Meaghan, a bright blue folder clutched in one hand, a gun in the other.

Linn pulled her Glock from her bag and exited the car, keeping the block wall between her and the other woman. "Drop the gun, Meaghan. Put your hands up."

She ignored the command, not moving.

"Meaghan Larson, hands up!" Linn cut a glance at Steve.

He shook his head and, at a crouch, headed around to come up behind Meaghan.

"My mother did care about me." Meaghan finally spoke and lifted her head. Tears ran down her cheeks. "She kept a file on her brother up until she killed him."

Linn hadn't located any file, and she thought she'd thoroughly searched the house. "Let us help you. Come with us. Detective Chavez—"

"Steve is here?" Meaghan whirled, putting the gun to her head. "It isn't time. Don't come any closer."

"Not time for what?" Linn asked. "Please put the gun down."

"No. If I do, you'll shoot me. If you come closer, I'll shoot myself and you'll never find Andrew. That's what I call him." She turned back to Linn. "A man should be called by his proper name. Next to Steve, Andrew is a wonderful man. Perhaps I'll keep them both. What do you say, cop lady? Will you give up your man to save his life?"

"Yes. In a heartbeat."

"Then, you'll let me walk away from you. Steve?"

"I'm here." He stepped from around the house, hands

held in front of him. "Let me come with you."

"Not yet. You come on my terms, Steve. Not because you happened upon me." She smiled. "There's no fun in that. I'll take you when you least expect it." She pressed the gun harder against her temple. "Both of you step back and let me leave, or I'll pull the trigger and those men will die."

Linn kept her gun aimed at Meaghan's head.

"Put it down, detective, or the chief dies first."

Steve stepped back. "Let her go, Linn. We'll get Drew another way."

Meaghan blew a kiss, dashed to the left, and hopped a short wall.

Linn fell to her knees. They'd almost had her.

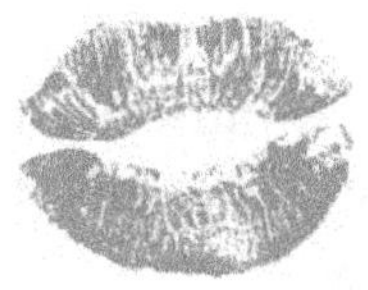

# Chapter Twenty-Two

It had taken all the willpower Steve possessed not to go after Meaghan. He wasn't one to usually listen to killers, but the man Linn loved was being held hostage. He couldn't do anything to risk Drew's life. Meaghan had said stay, and so he stayed.

"You should have stopped her." Linn hissed. "We could have forced her to tell us where Drew is."

"If she shot herself we'd never find them."

"She wouldn't have." Linn stormed back to his car.

"How do you know?" He jogged to catch up with her. "Were you willing to take that chance?" He grabbed her shoulders and spun her around. "Were you? What would you do if an action of yours resulted in Drew's death? I don't want to find out."

She slumped. "Neither do I. I guess you're the level-headed one right now."

Yeah. But he hadn't been when his twin brother had held Linn captive, obsessed with the woman he had raped.

Steve understood very well what Linn was going through.

She sat in the passenger seat staring out the window when he slid into the driver's seat. "I'm sorry."

She shrugged.

"Linn, look at me."

She turned with a stony face.

"I promise to do everything in my power to save Drew. That's all I can do."

Her features softened. "I know you will. I can only pray everyone is kept safe."

At least she included him in those she wanted to stay alive. Sometimes he wondered. Once, they'd been more than just partners, they'd been best friends, then, along came the handsome FBI agent in a cowboy hat and Linn transferred those affections somewhere else. Now that Drew was the chief, he was always around.

Not that Steve faulted Linn for falling for the guy. He would have if he were a woman. He smirked and drove them back to the station. Someday, a woman who wasn't a serial killer might fall in his path, and Steve could stop mourning what he couldn't have with Linn.

Back at the precinct, they headed to the conference room without speaking. Steve sighed. Linn might have said she understood, but she wasn't acting like she did.

"Where did you go?" Mayne looked up. "We got a tip Queen Coral was spotted at this address. We've sent a team."

Steve glanced at the note. "We were just there, and yes she was, too. She got away."

Linn made a sound in her throat. "She threatened to kill herself if we didn't let her go. So, Steve let her escape."

He shook his head. "We both put down our weapons."

"You should have grabbed her when her attention was focused on me."

"And let her shoot herself?"

"All right, children." Mayne frowned and glanced from

him to Linn. "I don't know what's going on between the two of you, but we have a group of men being held and, quite possibly, tortured. We need to come together. Linn, we'll get the chief back. Put your head back in your job and stop acting like a victim's hysterical wife."

Steve waited for Linn to explode. Instead, she said, "You're right. I'm sorry, Steve." She reached over and squeezed his hand, then turned back to Mayne. "What's next?"

"We wait for her to make her move." Mayne handed a small disc to Steve. "This is a tracker she won't be able to find."

"How so?" He studied the silver cylinder.

Mayne grinned. "Because the moment you know you're being taken, you're going to swallow it. It's only good until you, uh, pass it, so don't swallow until the last minute. We'll be able to track you up to fifty feet."

"That narrows down the search perimeter nicely." He slipped the device into his pocket. "Why didn't you give this to the chief?"

"I didn't have it. I had to call in a favor. No more questions about that."

~

Linn wished Mayne would have called in the favor sooner, so Drew could have had the device, but Steve was the next best thing. Once Meaghan took him, they'd have her in their clutches and behind bars. "Any other fancy spy gadgets that might help us?"

"Not really. If we knew where she was we could listen in or watch. Technology has gotten very good. But if you don't have a place to start…" She shrugged one shoulder.

"I understand." Linn approached the caseboard, studying the face of each man there, including Drew. Next to their picture was, their name, where they were taken, and ideas of why they were taken. All except Drew and Chang were because they had approached Meaghan, alledgedly, at a bar. All were handsome.

"We need information on Hank Larson." She stared at Meaghan's picture. "He's the key to all this."

"I agree." Mayne stood beside her. "All we know is he's her uncle, he abused her, and he died at the hands of Meaghan's mother. My guess is the man owns—" She rushed back to the table and ruffled through a file. "I know he owns land. Several hundred acres of heavily-wooded land, to be exact. What if he has a cabin up there that's never been recorded?"

Hope leaped in Linn. "A lot of people in these mountains live off the grid. It's quite possible. "I'll get a chopper in here. We didn't find anything the last time, but we can narrow our search. There has to be something we're missing." She grabbed her phone and placed a call for a chopper.

"I can't do that without the chief's signature."

"The chief is missing!" Seriously, some people were so fixated on the rules they couldn't see past their faces. "I'll take full responsibility, but we need your chopper to find him."

"I could get in trouble, detective."

"You'll be in jail if you don't stop obstructing justice."

"Fine. I'll have one ready within the hour."

"You'll have one ready now."

"Fine." Click.

"Let's go." Linn rushed out the door.

Fifteen minutes later, they were in the air, speeding across town to the mountain where Larson owned land. Mayne wasn't kidding. The trees were so thick Linn couldn't see anything. No smoke, no rooftop, no road.

"How would she get in there?" She glanced at Steve. "We know she drives a van. She can't possibly be carrying the men to a cabin."

He kept peering out the window. "There has to be some sort of road. Pilot, follow the road up the mountain. Let's see if we can see where something might branch off.”

“There’s all kinds of trails up here,” the pilot said. “I’ve hiked a lot of them. I’d guess there are several that a vehicle could get down if you don’t mind a bumpy ride. I don’t recall ever coming across a cabin this far out though.”

“Keep flying,” Linn said. “We’re missing something.” She had to be out here. A place in the city would increase her risk of being seen. The fact she had gone into town on a regular basis, though… “Who is Meaghan’s father?” She glanced at Steve. “Why has no one looked into him?”

“No one knows who he is,” Mayne explained. “Mom wasn’t exactly a pillar of virtue.”

What if they were on a wild goose chase? What if Meaghan had found out who her father was? Whether dead or alive the man could have left her a residence suitable for keeping a handful of prisoners.

“She isn’t out here.” Meaghan closed her eyes, nausea rising in her stomach. “She’s in the city somewhere. Head back.”

“Are you sure?” Steve put a hand on her arm.

She opened her eyes. “She worked in the city. She made regulars trips to the drugstore. This is too far.”

“One more pass on the edge of the land closest to town,” Mayne said. “Then, we’ll head back.”

Linn nodded. It was worth a try. “Then, as a last-ditch effort, fly over the part of town she frequented. Just in case.”

~

Drew jolted awake when a glass of ice water  was thrown in his face. He blinked and scowled. “What was that for?”

“For being right.” Meaghan pulled a chair close to him, her knees touching his. “Buried under the tree where I played as a child was a metal box. In that box was an envelope. In that envelope was my mother’s journal. She did love me. She did believe me. But my uncle was also abusing her physically, mentally, and sexually. From her notes, every time she tried to kill him, he would take it out on me. She wasn't able to succeed until I left."

"Why are you telling me this?"

"Maybe you aren't a typical, good-looking man full of lies." Her dark gaze pierced his. "I'd consider letting you go if I didn't think you'd arrest me."

"Smart move."

She laughed. "You don't like me very much, do you?"

"What's to like? You're very beautiful, Meaghan, but you're a heartless killer. There isn't much likeable about you."

She smiled. "You think I'm beautiful."

"You know you are. You use your looks to your advantage."

She stood, switching to sitting on his lap. She toyed with the few chest hairs he had. "You are brutally honest, chief. I like that. What would you do if I took you upstairs?"

"Absolutely nothing." And he meant nothing. He'd learned a long time ago to make his body behave when he needed it to.

"Pity." She yanked out a hair. "We could have a good time, you and I."

"Ow."

She sighed and got up. "The rest of these men participate. Not one of them has complained. If you won't play with me, I'll take Agent Chang."

Drew glanced at the agent, who shrugged. "He might be willing if you don't try hurting him again."

She slapped him hard enough to turn his head. "You don't give the orders here. I do. Nor do you give permission for anyone I choose to play with. Agent Chang will cooperate or regret it." She put a hand on each arm of his chair and leaned forward.

His gaze flicked to the loose-fitting blouse which gaped

open giving him a nice view, then back to her face. "Why not let the man decide for himself? If you don't want my opinion, don't ask for it."

"Oh, you are a naughty boy." She grabbed his face and planted a heated kiss on his lips. "You might want to reconsider. Eventually, you'll have to make a choice. Give in or die."

"Do you want my decision now?"

"Hush, bad boy. I'm going to go play now." She retrieved the ever-present gun from the drawer, cursing because Sharon had left the cabinet unlocked, then aimed it in Drew's direction while she released Chang's legs. "Come along nicely, agent, or I kill him."

"I'll come." He shot Drew a look that clearly said he'd take the opportunity to rid them of Meaghan if it presented itself.

Drew couldn't help but hope it would. He wouldn't willingly betray Linn under any circumstances. Instinct told him Meaghan would soon test him. What if he failed?

Without a clock, he didn't know how long Chang was gone and had fallen asleep, only to be awakened by an unearthly scream.

"Man, he did something wrong," Jamal said, shaking his head. "Why can't you guys listen to us?"

"What is she doing to him?" Drew kept his gaze locked on the door above the stairs.

"Torturing him. It excites her."

Drew closed his eyes and prayed.

Quite a while longer, helped by Sharon, Meaghan brought Chang back to the basement. The man could hardly walk. If not for the women under his arm, he would have fallen.

Meaghan tied him back to his chair. "Take a good look, fellas. This is what happens when you try to hurt me." She swiped the back of her hand against a bloody lip, grinned, and left.

Drew swallowed hard and glanced at Chang. A raw, oozing burn ran from the conclave at the base of his throat to the band of his undershorts.

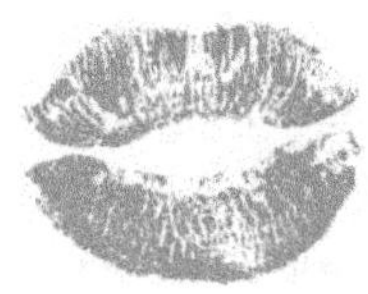

# Chapter Twenty-Three

"Chang, can you hear me?" Drew used his bound feet to hop the chair closer.

"Yeah, I hear you." He lifted his head. "That was a bad idea."

"You okay?"

He nodded. "I will be. She was nice enough to pour whiskey on the burn to disinfect it. What is this? The eighteenth century?"

Primitive, but effective. "What happened?"

He grinned. "After we did the two-sheet tango, I flipped her off the bed and made a lunge for the gun. I didn't know she had a Taser under the pillow." He glared at the others. "That piece of information would have been nice to know. She got me down and finished what she'd started yesterday. The only good that came out of all this was I got a shower first thing."

"I didn't know about the Taser," Jamal said.

The others shook their heads.

"You're lucky she didn't kill you," Drew said. Why was she keeping them alive? Was it only until she had

175

Steve? Were they really nothing more than toys to keep her amused? If so, the woman was more deranged than he'd thought. "What did you see up there?"

"It's an old house. I could hear sounds of traffic, a distant siren, but nothing to tell me where we are. All I know is we're in town."

Drew nodded. Eventually someone would spot Meaghan again and draw Linn and the others closer to rescuing them. "Where is Sharon's guy?"

"He's locked in another room unless he's with Sharon. He has more freedom than we do, but the man is still a prisoner."

Drew stared at the floor between his knees. All Chang's efforts showed was that they were within city limits. That didn't help when zip ties kept them firmly secured to chairs. It was only a matter of time before Drew was taken upstairs. What could he do up there to free them?

Even he wouldn't be able to move if tased. He'd have to take her down before reaching the bedroom. Which meant, he'd have to get the gun away from her. With his hands tied and his feet free. It was possible.

"Hello, boys." Meaghan skipped down the stairs. "My love will be here soon. I have everything in place." She tapped her finger against her lips.

A move Drew had come to dread. It meant she was thinking of her next atrocity. "Your collection will be complete."

"I'll actually have more than I need." She stared at David.

"The more men you have, the more compliant Steve will be." Drew met her stare with an unblinking one of his own. "The very thing you love about him will be what keeps him pliable. Steve will do whatever you ask if it means the life of one of these men will be saved."

She nodded, a slow smile spreading across her face. "You are absolutely right. Why, his kindness and caring for others will make him putty in my hands. Well done, chief. You just saved these mens' lives." She clapped. "I guess that makes you a hero."

Hardly. If he were a hero, they'd be home with their families by now.

Meaghan patted his cheek. "See you later." She tweaked his nose and dashed up the stairs.

~

"I have news of Meaghan Larson. Meet me at the corner of Third and Maple." Click.

Linn hung up the phone and stared at the receiver. It could be another prank call. They'd gone on quite a few wild goose chases the last few days, but the voice sounded familiar.

"Who was it?" Steve glanced up from his desk.

"Another call about Meaghan. Except, I think we should check this one out. I'm not sure, but the voice sounded like Sharon Morrall."

He frowned. "Would she put herself in danger for Meaghan?"

"I think the woman would do anything for her psycho cousin." Linn stood and grabbed her shoulder holster. "Got the tracker?"

He nodded slowly. "You think this is it?"

"I do." Her heart stuttered. While she didn't love Steve the same way he did her, he was very dear to her. If something happened to him, there would be a gaping hole in her life. "Be careful. Do what she says."

"I will." He shrugged into his suit jacket. "It isn't only my life at stake here."

"I'm sorry if I made it seem as if your life didn't matter." She put a hand on his arm. "I'd like both of my men to come home."

"I'll do my best."

She followed him to her car, then got in the driver's seat. Without another word, she started the car and drove to

Third and Maple. Alan Barker, pain-in-the-rear reporter, rushed toward them. Linn frowned and pushed open her door. "How did you know to come here?"

"An anonymous tip. The person said if I came here, I'd have a story."

"You should leave, Alan. It isn't safe."

"I've been in dangerous situations before."

What kind of story was he called in for? Fingers of dread walked up Linn's spine. "I think we need to call for backup. I don't like this. Other than us and the camera crew, no one is here."

"I agree," Steve said. "This isn't what I expected."

Linn neither. She'd expected to see the white van, either Sharon or Meaghan, and hear an order for Steve to go with them. This eerie silence was unnerving. "Where are all the people? This area is usually crowded with shoppers."

Spotting an elderly man peering from the barred door of a video store, she marched over to him. When he ducked out of sight, she knocked and showed her badge. "Sir?"

"Go away."

"I need you to tell me why everyone is hiding."

He peeked out. "Some sort of explosion occurred about fifteen minutes before you arrived. Then, the street filled with smoke. It's all gone now, but no one wants to come out until the area is deemed safe."

Why in the world would Meaghan set off a smoke bomb? She glanced at Steve, who shrugged. "Thank you, sir. Please remain inside where it's safe."

Linn's cell phone rang the same time someone stepped into the intersection. Sharon Morrall held a phone to one ear and what looked like a remote in the other. Linn pressed the green button on her cell phone. "Hello, Sharon."

"Detective."

"Are you here to give yourself up? We understand you were forced into helping Meaghan. She's a very formidable person."

"She's family." Sharon took a few steps closer. When Linn started to do the same, she said, "I wouldn't if I were you. Detective Chavez, please come with me. If you resist, the consequences will not be pretty."

Sirens wailed in the distance. "You called for backup?" Sharon pressed the remote. An ice cream parlor at the end of the street exploded. Debris rained down on Linn, Steve, and the camera crew. "No one else was supposed to come. Why isn't the film crew taping?"

Alan motioned for the camera to start filming.

"Where is Martin?" Linn straightened.

"He's standing ready to finish our mission if I should fail."

Steve stepped forward. "How can you fail? I told Meaghan I would come willingly."

She smiled. "You know her. She likes to make a statement. Call off your backup, or I press this button again. We've set every building on this side of the street to explode."

No wonder they wanted all the people inside. Linn placed the call.

"We can't do that," Mayne said.

"Dozens of people will die if you don't call it off." Linn held Sharon's gaze.

"I'll turn off the siren. SWAT will come in undetected. They'll have to take her out, Linn. There's no other choice."

"Thank you." Linn hung up as the sirens ceased. "They're turning back. You won."

Martin joined Sharon in the intersection. He wore a vest covered with explosives. He aimed a gun at Alan. The look on his face clearly stated he had no choice but to do as ordered. Not if he wanted to live.

Things were not going to end well for either Sharon or Martin.

Steve stepped closer, hands held high. "I'm coming. There's no need for further loss of life."

Linn hadn't seen him swallow the tracker. *Please, swallow it.*

"There is a white van around the corner," Sharon said. "Get in it. If you aren't in when I get there, I'll blow another building."

"No need. I'll be there." Steve kept walking. Once he was past Sharon and Martin, Linn saw him slip his hand into his pocket, then into his mouth.

Thank you, God.

"Now back up, Detective McFarland." Sharon started walking backward, same as Martin.

A shot rang out.

Sharon fell.

Another building blew, along with Martin.

Steve crumbled to the ground.

Linn fell to her knees. "No!" All their plans, all their work, was for nothing. "Steve."

A white van careened around the corner, stopping next to Steve. Meaghan got out, grabbed his feet and dragged him to the back of the van. When Linn got to her feet, the woman shook her head no and pulled a gun from the pocket of her jacket. She aimed at Alan and pulled the trigger.

Alan yelled and folded to the ground.

SWAT and firetrucks roared onto the street. Personnel poured from the vehicles like ants from an anthill. One of the SWAT team members knelt and aimed a weapon at the van.

Linn waved her arms. "No. Let them go."

Meaghan tossed something out of the van window as she drove away.

Linn checked on Alan, relieved to discover the bullet had gone through his shoulder. The cameraman hadn't been so lucky. The explosion of the building behind him hadn't left much of the man.

"Why?" Alan shook his head. "A senseless waste of life because of one man. It doesn't make sense."

"No, it doesn't." How could Meaghan be so fixated on Steve that she would kill so many innocent people? He had told her he would go willingly. Why the dramatics?

She went to retrieve what Meaghan had tossed out the window. It was a small white cylinder big enough for an 8 ½ x 11 sheet of paper. Inside was a photo of Drew tied to a chair, wearing nothing but his underwear and a belligerent expression. On the back of the photo was written, "I hope you liked the fireworks. This was intended as a warning not to come looking for your men. They are mine now."

"We shall see." Linn traced Drew's face. "I'm coming, sweetheart."

"You're bleeding." Mayne handed her a towel and pointed to her head. "Flying glass."

"Thanks." Linn dabbed the spot, handing Mayne the photo. "This was all a warning to stop looking for her."

"It'll be a nightmare trying to find out who the victims in the shops are." Mayne shook her head. "I've never seen anything like this woman before." She sighed. "A package on Hank Larson is being sent to the office. Do you need to be checked out by the paramedics first?"

"No, I'm fine." Linn turned and headed for the car. "Let's find this witch and save our guys."

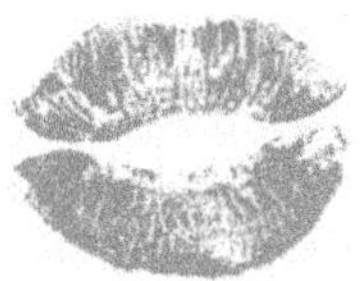

# Chapter Twenty-Four

Steve opened his eyes and stifled a groan. Glancing around him, he was able to determine that he was stripped to his underwear, tied up like a Thanksgiving turkey, and tossed into the back of a panel van. The last thing he remembered was an explosion. The concussion had knocked him down.

He couldn't be positive, but he didn't think they'd driven very far before stopping. The sound of a garage door closing reached him through the van walls. Seconds later, the back doors opened.

"Darling!" Meaghan grabbed his bound hands and pulled him to a sitting position. "With that knot on your head, I feared you might not wake up."

He blinked against the light streaming through the garage window. "Why all the drama, Meaghan? You killed innocent people. I told you I would come willingly."

"I know, but it wouldn't have been near as much fun." She grinned and led him like a cow to slaughter into a simple, ranch-style home. "I did have a flicker of sadness at seeing my cousin fall."

The woman's madness was escalating. Steve saw it in

her dark eyes. A tender thread kept her tethered to reality. That knowledge scared him more than if he were looking down the barrel of a gun.

"Am I going to have trouble with you?" She tilted her head, staring into his face.

"No." He smiled, stepping closer. Steve wasn't adept at the art of flirtation, but his life and the lives of the others depended on her trusting him, believing he was infatuated with her. "Unless you want trouble."

A slow smile stretched her lips. She really was a beautiful woman. A pity she'd spend the rest of her life behind bars.

"I would love to believe the vibe you're giving out," she said. "But I'll err on the side of caution and lock you with the others until I can be sure." She got on her tiptoes and kissed him, her lips lingering. "I've missed you."

"If you untied me, I could wrap my arms around you and show you how much I've missed you."

She laughed and playfully slapped his chest. "Patience, sweetheart." She gripped the tie holding his hands together and led him down a flight of stairs.

The others were lined up in mis-matched chairs, following their movement as Meaghan brought him down. Steve gave Drew a small nod, receiving nothing but an impassive stare in return. Still, Steve detected a flicker of hope in the other man's eyes.

The odor of unwashed bodies and fear hung heavy in the air. Meaghan led Steve to a chair with a padded seat. "I guess I'm priviledged," he said.

"Until you give me reason otherwise." She caressed his cheek, then bound his ankles to the legs of the chair. "I look forward to our time together." Another hot and heavy kiss, then she left the men alone.

"Are you all right?" Steve asked Drew.

"I'm fine. It seems that, next to you, I'm the next in line to be her favorite. Tell me you have a way to get us out of here."

"I do. Be patient. It will take a little time for Linn to find us, but it shouldn't be later than tonight." If the tracker could penetrate the concrete walls. Surely the FBI had thought of that. He noticed the burn on Chang's chest. "Did Meaghan do that?"

"Yep, because I knocked her to the floor and bloodied her lip." He grinned. "But not until I had a little fun."

Steve turned away. The idea that he'd had sex with a woman who used men as if they were things to be tossed aside made his stomach churn. Multiple men. He shuddered, knowing he might very well have to participate again to stay alive.

"I'm sorry, man," Drew said in that uncanny way he had of reading someone's mind. "I know you thought she was the one."

"Until we get out of here, she is the one." He pulled against his bindings. He wasn't going anywhere. "Sharon and the man she took are both dead. Meaghan is hanging on, mentally, by a thread."

Drew nodded. "We're all doing our best to behave."

Steve grinned. "That must stick in your craw."

"It does. Linn handling things okay?"

"Better than I thought. She needs you home, though." Steve studied the faces of the other men. While they met his gaze, the lack of hope and the spirit of dejection filled them. He wanted to tell them they'd all get out alive. He prayed they would. But with a deranged person like Meaghan, that was a promise he might not be able to keep.

~

"He's here, he's here," Meaghan sang as she danced around her bedroom, yanking sheets from the bed. No more men in her room. The one she wanted had arrived. She really should kill the others, but kind-hearted Steve would most likely never forgive her. Perhaps he was right about the useless dramatics of the explosions. She shrugged. No use crying over what couldn't be changed.

Tonight needed to be special. She'd fix a wonderful supper, light some candles, and have a night with Steve like they used to. Before everything went awry. Still, she had no one to blame but herself. Even while seeing Steve, she'd taken other men to play with. It was an addiction she needed to break…*would* break.

She remade the bed with fresh sheets and headed for the kitchen. What she wouldn't give to be able to go back to her modern, stylish apartment. This house hadn't been renovated since the seventies. Still, no one expected a woman like her to be living in such simple surroundings.

Meaghan chose Italian food—spaghetti, garlic bread, salad and wine. A romantic dinner for the man she came as close to loving as was possible for her shattered heart. Uncle Hank had done a number on her, that was for sure. But now…she had a man that might be able to put the pieces back together. They could leave the country and start over in a new place. Maybe start a family.

Her mind swirled with possibilities, her heart swelled with hope. The future looked brighter than it had in a long time.

~

Linn spread the file on Hank Larson across the table. "How long until we get a track on Steve?"

"Within the hour. The techs want to make sure he's in one spot. The signal keeps blinking in and out. They'll let us know as soon as he's pinpointed," Mayne said. "Then we'll join SWAT and rescue the men."

"This whole process takes too long." Maybe there was something in Larson's file that would allow them to bypass waiting on the technicians. Bingo! "Larson owned a house downtown."

"I'll see whether someone has been using utilities." Mayne grinned and grabbed the phone. Five minutes later, she said, "We've got her. Someone is using water and electricity from that address. Someone under the name of Mary Larson."

"I bet that person doesn't exist." Linn clutched the paper with the address. "Call SWAT. I want out of here asap."

Twenty minutes later they hunkered behind a non-descript utility van and stared at a one-story, ranch-style brick home. The grass had long since died, leaving more packed dirt than weeds. Curtains were drawn tight behind windows. No bushes softened the front landscape.

"I'm going to peek in the garage," Linn said. "See if her van is there."

"Even if it isn't, Detective Chavez is," a male technician smiled through the open side door of the van. "We had some trouble with the tracker. It might have been damaged in the explosion, but it's working now."

"That's the best thing I've heard since we started this case." Keeping low, Linn jogged for the garage. Sure enough, the white van she'd seen Steve leave in was parked inside.

She continued around the back of the house and tried to peer in one of the slim windows close to the ground. Some sort of blackout paper covered each of the windows. No way to be certain, but the basement was the best place for Meaghan to keep the men. Hadn't Bill Nelson said he climbed out a basement window when he escaped? There. A window, boarded up with slabs of wood.

Linn pressed her eye against a small separation in the wood. All eight of the men were accounted for and alive. She sagged with relief to see Drew and Steve talking. She couldn't hear what was being said, but would bet her Kevlar vest they were making plans to escape. She returned to the others.

"Prisoners are tied to chairs in the basement. No way in but through one of the doors in the house." She took a deep breath. "I suggest we wait for cover of darkness. Move this van further down the street. The last thing we want to do is make Meaghan suspicious."

Mayne waved her arm, motioning the vehicles to move back. "Hang tight for a couple of hours, folks.

Finally they would put an end to the nightmare that was Meaghan Larson. What had to snap in someone's head to turn them into such a vicious killer? Meaghan wasn't the first person to be abused as a child, used as a woman. But then, her mother had seemed to have a screw loose of her own. Mental illness ran through the family, it seemed.

"Coffee?" Mayne handed her a styrofoam cup. "It's going to be a long two hours."

"Yeah." Linn took a sip. "Why'd you get into law enforcement?"

"My father was a cop. My grandfather was a cop. It seemed the logical choice. You?"

"Orphaned at a young age because of murder. Danced to earn the money to go through the academy and college. I wanted to see justice done. Sometimes, I wonder what I was thinking."

Mayne laughed without humor. "I get it. The things we see…the atrocities man can do to each other." She shook her head, her smile fading. "I thought I'd seen it all, but this case is right up there as one of the worse."

~

"Hungry?" Meaghan cut Steve's ankles away from the chair legs. "I've a shirt and jacket for you to wear. It's bad manners not to come to the dinner table dressed."

"Why strip us to our underwear in the first place?"

"It makes you vulnerable. Come on." She led him upstairs then, alternated handcuffing each of his hands to the table leg so he could dress.

A starched-white tablecloth covered a table. On top were a set of fine white china he recognized from a time he'd eaten at her apartment. Wine glasses—two for each of them, one containing red wine, the other white—stood next to the plates. The only light came from the three pillar candles in the center of the table. "It's beautiful, and the food smells great." His traitorous stomach growled. "I love Italian."

"I know." She smiled and took her seat next to him. She looked ravishing in a coral-colored dress that matched the infamous lipstick on her lips.

Again, he couldn't help but think what if she was a psycho?

"Does your head hurt? That bump is turning a nice shade of purple, and you're frowning." She lifted a glass of red wine to her mouth.

"A bit."

"I'm sorry you were caught up in all that. I didn't mean for you to be injured." She reached over and placed her hand on his. "Let's go away from here. We could go to Mexico and live like royalty. The tropical parts are quite beautiful."

"What about the others?"

"I suppose you would want me to release them?"

He nodded. "I'll follow you to the ends of the earth if you'll let them go."

She sighed heavily and stared at him over the rim of her glass as she took another sip. "Don't you ever think only of yourself?"

"Not really. That's why I became a police officer." He took a bite out of his garlic bread, grateful it wasn't his right hand cuffed to the table. Where was Linn?

"Hmmm." She set her glass down and twirled her fork in her spaghetti. "I went to a lot of trouble to take those—"

The dining room window shattered. A bang and a bright light rendered Steve momentarily deaf and blind.

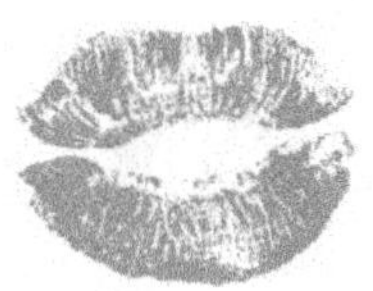

# Chapter Twenty-Five

"No!" Meaghan crawled to Steve, held him in front of her, and pointed the gun to his head. "Not you, too. You betrayed me just like the rest."

"Never. I've been here with you. How could I have let them know where we are?" He peered up into her tear-streaked face. "Unlock the cuffs. We have to get out of here." He cupped her cheek with his free hand and forced the words, "I love you. Let's go before it's too late."

"Do you mean it?"

"Yes."

She uncuffed him, and before he could move, put the other cuff around her wrist. Keeping the gun trained on him, she practically dragged him out the backdoor. "Don't shoot. I will kill him."

Steve held up his hand to stop the SWAT team from firing. The longer he could convince Meaghan he meant his declaration of love, the better chance he had of getting out of this alive.

"Steve." Linn's cry ripped at his heart.

"Don't look back," Meaghan said. "It's her or me."

"Keep running."

She squeezed his hand and darted across the two-lane road running behind her house. "I keep another vehicle back here."

"You've thought of everything."

Once they were out of danger of innocent people dying because of her wild shots, Steve yanked her arm, pulling her against his chest. With his arm across her neck, he squeezed. "I really did think you were the one." He kept up the pressure until she sagged unconscious and dropped the gun. After a frantic search for the handcuff key, he found it stashed in her bra.

He freed himself, handcuffed her hands behind her, then lifted her in his arms and headed back to the house.

~

"Drew." Linn thundered down the basement stairs. "I'm here." She cut through the zip ties holding him and threw her arms around his neck. "Tell me you're okay."

"I'm fine. She didn't hurt me. Chang needs medical attention, though. How did you find us?"

She cupped his face. "Steve swallowed a tracker."

"Where is he?"

"She took him. Can you walk?" She helped him to his feet while Mayne released the other men. "Lean on me if you have to."

She escorted him outside to a waiting ambulance, then stood back and searched the surrounding buildings for a sign of Steve. "Did anyone see which direction they went?"

"Out the backdoor," a SWAT member said. "They were handcuffed together. I didn't hear any gunshots."

Relief flooded through Linn. Steve still had a chance.

"Go," Drew said. "I'll be fine. Look for Steve."

"I love you." She gave him a kiss. "I love him, too. He's been my bestfriend for a long time."

He nodded. "Go, honey. I'll be waiting here for you. If I had clothes, I'd help you look."

She kissed him again and took off in a run in the direction the team member thought they'd gone. She burst between two houses, coming out onto a tree-lined street. Coming toward her was Steve, barefoot, wearing boxer shorts and a suit jacket. In his arms he carried Meaghan. Linn hurried toward them. "What happened?"

"I got away."

"Is she dead?"

He shook his head. "No, she's unconscious and will be waking up soon." He continued his walk toward the others.

"Are you all right?" Linn walked backwards in front of him, keeping her gaze locked on his.

"I'm fine. No, I'm not. My heart is breaking. I really did care for this woman before I found out she was Queen Coral." His green eyes shimmered. "Why can't I find someone like you?"

"You will. I know you will." She put up a hand to stop him. "I'm sorry I can't love you the way you want me to."

He shrugged. "The heart does what it wants. Drew is a lucky man. Maybe I'm meant to be alone."

Linn fell into step next to him. "She's waking up." Linn trained her weapon on Meaghan as Steve set her on her feet.

"Just as I thought." Meaghan spit in his face. "You're no different than the rest of them."

"I'm very much different." Steve turned her to face where they wanted to go and gave her a push to get her started.

"What does she have that I don't?" She motioned her head at Linn.

"Morals for one," Linn said. "A respect for human life. I could go on, but somehow I think your question was rhetorical."

Meaghan cursed and tried to head-butt Steve. He gave her another shove.

"I'll come for you when I get out, Steve Chavez. This

isn't the end of us."

"Sweetheart, you won't be getting out. You'll rot in prison for the crimes you've done."

When they joined the others, and Meaghan was stashed in the back of a squad car, Linn watched as Steve donned a pair of scrub bottoms and talked to Mayne. Perhaps, at a later date, she could convince the two of them to go out to dinner together. Mayne would need time to mourn the loss of her partner, but the tall blond next to the dark-haired Steve made a nice pair.

"What are you thinking?" Drew wrapped his arms around her waist from behind.

"That they would make a nice pair."

"I never took you for a matchmaker."

"I've never seen Steve this downtrodden." She turned and stared into the face of the man she loved. "He was risking his life for you just because I asked him to."

"It's no secret how he feels about you."

She nodded and stepped into his arms. "I need a vacation from all this."

He chuckled, his chest vibrating under her cheek. "That sounds like a wonderful idea."

The End

Stay Tuned for the final book in the Colors of Evil series, Indigo Nightmares

# ABOUT THE AUTHOR

Website at www.cynthiahickey.com

Also www.forgetmenotromances.com

Multi-published and Amazon and ECPA Best-Selling author Cynthia Hickey has sold over a million copies of her works since 2013. She has taught a Continuing Education class at the 2015 American Christian Fiction Writers conference, several small ACFW chapters and RWA chapters. You can find her on FB, twitter, and Goodreads, and is a contributor to Cozy Mystery Magazine blog and Suspense Sisters blog. She and her husband run the small press, Forget Me Not Romances, which includes some of the CBA's best well-known authors. She lives in Arizona with her husband, one of their seven children, two dogs, one cat, and three box turtles. She has eight grandchildren who keep her busy and tell everyone they know that "Nana is a writer".

Connect with me on FaceBook
Twitter
Amazon
Sign up for my newsletter and receive a free 14 author serial romance
www.cynthiahickey.com

Follow me on Amazon

Enjoy other books by Cynthia Hickey

**Shady Acres Mysteries**
Beware the Orchids, book 1

<u>Path to Nowhere</u>
<u>Poison Foliage</u>
<u>Poinsettia Madness</u>
<u>Deadly Greenhouse Gases</u>
<u>Vine Entrapment</u>

## INSPIRATIONAL
(scroll down to see clean books without inspirational message)

Nosy Neighbor Series
<u>Anything For A Mystery</u>, Book 1
<u>A Killer Plot</u>, Book 2
<u>Skin Care Can Be Murder</u>, Book 3
<u>Death By Baking</u>, Book 4
<u>Jogging Is Bad For Your Health</u>, Book 5
<u>Poison Bubbles</u>, Book 6
<u>A Good Party Can Kill You</u>, Book 7 (Final)
<u>Nosy Neighbor collection</u>

<u>Christmas with Stormi Nelson</u>

**The Summer Meadows Series**
<u>Fudge-Laced Felonies</u>, Book 1
<u>Candy-Coated Secrets</u>, Book 2
<u>Chocolate-Covered Crime</u>, Book 3
<u>Maui Macadamia Madness</u>, Book 4
<u>All four novels in one collection</u>

**The River Valley Mystery Series**
<u>Deadly Neighbors</u>, Book 1
<u>Advance Notice</u>, Book 2
<u>The Librarian's Last Chapter</u>, Book 3
<u>All three novels in one collection</u>

**Historical cozy**
<u>Hazel's Quest</u>

**Historical Romances**
**Runaway Sue**
Taming the Sheriff
Sweet Apple Blossom

**Finding Love the Harvey Girl Way**
Cooking With Love
Guiding With Love
Serving With Love
Warring With Love
All 4 in 1

A Wild Horse Pass Novel
They Call Her Mrs. Sheriff, book 1 (A Western Romance)

Finding Love in Disaster
The Rancher's Dilemma
The Teacher's Rescue
The Soldier's Redemption

Woman of courage Series

A Love For Delicious
Ruth's Redemption
Charity's Gold Rush
Mountain Redemption
Woman of Courage series (all four books)

Short Story Westerns
Desert Rose
Desert Lilly
Desert Belle
Desert Daisy
Flowers of the Desert 4 in 1

**Romantic Suspense**

Overcoming Evil series
Mistaken Assassin

Captured Innocence
Mountain of Fear
Exposure at Sea
A Secret to Die for
Collision Course
Romantic Suspense of 5 books in 1

The Game
Suspicious Minds

**Contemporary**

**Romance in Paradise**
Maui Magic
Sunset Kisses
Deep Sea Love
3  in 1

Finding a Way Home

Service of Love

**Christmas**

Handcarved Christmas
The Payback Bride
Curtain Calls and Christmas Wishes
Christmas Gold
A Christmas Stamp

**The Red Hat's Club (Contemporary novellas)**

Finally
Suddenly
Surprisingly
The Red Hat's Club 3 – in 1

**CLEAN BUT GRITTY**

Colors of Evil Series

Shades of Crimson

The Pretty Must Die Series

Ripped in Red, book 1
Pierced in Pink, book 2
Wounded in White, book 3
Worthy, The Complete Story

Lisa Paxton Mystery Series

Eenie Meenie Miny Mo
Jack Be Nimble
Hickory Dickory Dock

One Hour (A short story thriller)